D0594520

THE LAST
SNAKE RUNNER

KIMBERLEY GRIFFITHS LITTLE

LAUREL-LEAF BOOKS

Published by
Dell Laurel-Leaf
an imprint of
Random House Children's Books
a division of Random House, Inc.
New York

Visit us on the Web! www.randomhouse.com/teens

Educators and librarians, for a variety of teaching tools, visit us at www.randomhouse.com/teachers

ISBN: 0-440-23782-3

RL: 5.3

Reprinted by arrangement with Alfred A. Knopf

Printed in the United States of America

First Dell Laurel-Leaf Edition November 2004

10 9 8 7 6 5 4 3 2 1

OPM

This book is for my parents, who never
turned out the light on reading,
just took me to the library again.
In memory of my father, Keith Griffiths,
for the legacy of becoming a writer, which was
one of his own dreams cut short,
and for my wonderful, loving mother, Dorothy Griffiths,
who gave me life and has been my example of strength
and devotion in so many ways.

ACKNOWLEDGMENTS

would like to thank my dear friend Carmel Keyope, her sons, Jonathan, David, and Michael, as well as Carmel's extended family for their friendship and generosity in sharing their life, their dancing, and meals around the table in one of the most enchanting spots on this earth.

Great appreciation goes to my agent, Irene Kraas, for loving this story and working hard to find the right home for it; gratitude also to my editor, Nancy Hinkel, for her enthusiastic dedication to this book, as well as her delight in the magic of the Snake Runners.

Simple words of appreciation aren't enough for my wonderful husband, Rusty, and my three great sons, Aaron, Jared, and Adam, who have journeyed with me along the trail of this dream. You are all such a blessing in my life. And special thanks to Jared for thinking up such a great title!

Thanks to Kendall, my youngest brother, for not minding that I used his name, which I've always loved.

PROLOGUE

ndall drank the bitter brew, trying not to gag when his
oat closed. In a few minutes he would vomit, and the
ansing process would be finished.

Piñon smoke and sweating bodies filled the sacred kiva
amber. Barefoot and wearing his deerskin breechcloth, Ken-
ll shuffled across the smooth rock floor, following the other
ncers. Drummers knelt beside the altar, and the steady
unding sound filtered through the opening in the roof.
e gentle rhythm rocked Kendall's heart like a baby in a
dle.

There was no other place he would rather have been.

From the head of the circle, the medicine man took the
oden bowl of herbs from Kendall's hands.

"Your great-grandfather would be proud," the elderly man
d solemnly. "But as the last Snake Runner, you will have
lifficult journey."

Kendall nodded. "He told me there were snake dances in
e ancient days."

The elderly man looked into Kendall's eyes. "The old
ys are lost to us. We must rely on the gods to guide you."

Before Kendall could speak again, the medicine man
ised a hand to signal the last dance.

Joining the boys from the other clans who were also be-
g initiated into the kiva ways, Kendall lifted his feet for

the final song to the gods. Bells around his ankles jangl
softly. Prayer sticks and smoothly carved bear bones clatter
at his waist, keeping time with the ancient drumbeats. Th
day was the final step in becoming a full member of the trib

The kiva chamber was filled with fathers, brothers, u
cles, and grandfathers from each of the village clans. The
were there to watch their sons on this important day. Bea
Antelope, Corn, and Eagle—more than a dozen clans. Ke
dall was still learning them all. But he was the only memb
of the Snake Clan.

Kendall wished Armando, his great-grandfather, we
there dancing beside him in breechcloth and eagle feathe
his long white hair majestic in the firelight.

Nobody spoke. The singers sang, the drums pounde
feet dusted the stone in steps that were centuries old. Ke
dall suddenly scanned the chamber, sensing those eyes th
watched him from the spirit world. Armando and Kendal
mother observed his dancing, listened to him speak Ker
san. He always felt their presence when he was here
Acoma. He wasn't completely alone.

The center fire crackled, throwing shadows onto th
adobe walls. Paintings of rain gods and bolts of lightning l
up under the fire's yellow glow. Through the doorway in th
roof, stars sparkled from an inky desert sky.

The other boys turned in a circle around the fire, and a
they danced their bodies became a single watery outlin
Kendall resisted the urge to wipe his eyes, then realize
there were no tears. The forms of bodies, fire, altar, and kiv
walls were merging and shifting. He brushed back his lor
black hair. The room began to spin.

The entire kiva chamber, as well as every man there, began to dissolve and disappear. Kendall lurched and fell toward the fire. The hair on his arms singed, and he felt a sharp burning. The room turned black, like a night without stars or moon.

Then the bottom of the world fell away, swallowing him whole.

Firelight pricked his eyelids, and when Kendall opened his eyes, he saw the stone ceiling overhead and recognized the paintings on the kiva walls.

Sweat trickled down his face and ran like warm water into his ears. How much time had passed? He was sure days had gone by—or had it been only minutes?

Several warriors bent over him. He saw a black night through the roof's opening, but the drums were now silent.

"Is he sick from the emetic?" a voice said in the Keresan language.

"There is no vomit," another voice answered.

"Look at his eyes," a boy said.

The deep voice of the medicine man said, "He has seen a vision."

"How long has he been fasting?" an elderly man asked, coming closer.

The crowd of bodies came into focus, and Kendall could see one of the oldest drummers kneeling over him in his leather breechcloth.

The medicine man spoke again from somewhere near Kendall's feet. "Two weeks. The boy is determined to be a good warrior. Even at night when he's allowed to eat, he barely fills his belly during this fasting period."

"He must be ill," the first voice said.

"No, he is not ill," the elder replied softly as he watched Kendall's face. "I think the spirit world has spoken to him."

"No more talking," the medicine man commanded. "Help him to his feet."

Arms escorted Kendall to the stone seat built into the circular walls. He was ashamed to have collapsed like that, as if he'd fainted. But they said he hadn't been sick. In fact, his stomach gurgled with the emetic brew sloshing at the pit of his belly.

"What day is it?" he asked.

"It's not a new day, boy. It is the same night."

"Perhaps he has traveled to a place where time stands still," said the older man.

The group retreated, but Kendall felt every eye studying him.

It felt like he'd been gone for days instead of just moments. The kiva floor had dropped out from under his feet and taken him to another time. A time when some kind of presence overshadowed everything. Something sinister that lurked and spilled into every corner of Acoma. Even the corners of this sacred kiva. But how could that be? No ordinary men were allowed here. This was the kiva where Kendall had learned the Acoma tribal ways, the Keresan language, and the stories of Creation. This was also the place where he had passed his initiation and been welcomed as one of the clansmen, part of them at last. His great-grandfather's dying wish had been fulfilled, but now that Armando was gone, Kendall was the last member of the Snake Clan. The last Snake Runner.

It was a hot, sweaty July night, but Kendall felt cold. Coldness like he'd never felt before, deep inside his soul, that made him ache. Armando had bestowed his Snake Runner power onto Kendall that night he lay dying on the desert, but Kendall couldn't stop thinking about how the powerful running magic carried by the Snake Clan would die whenever Kendall died.

Kendall followed the dancers and drummers as they filed out to retch over the cliffs and finish the cleansing. Afterward, they would return to their families to close the fasting with a huge feast.

As he walked along the edge of the cliff, Kendall shivered in the hot summer air. He knelt and looked down the sheer walls of pink and cream-colored stone. A bed of boulders lay at the bottom of the desert floor four hundred feet below. The end of summer was coming too soon, and Kendall knew he would be sent home again, back to reality and school and his other life.

He fingered the turquoise necklace at the base of his throat. Emotion tugged at his face. Digging into the sacred bundle at his waist, Kendall pulled out a prayer stick that he'd carved into a wriggling snake. He smoothed his hands along the shape of the piñon wood reptile, then touched it lightly with his lips.

"Grandfather, I promise I will always run with all my heart."

When he knew he was alone at the mesa's edge, Kendall tied back his long hair and threw up in private.

CHAPTER
ONE

Kendall knew evil existed in the universe, and ever since the night the kiva floor had swallowed him, he'd had sweaty, sick-to-his-stomach nightmares reminding him it was still there. Two weeks later he shot up in bed, gasping, knowing he'd been screaming in his dream.

The hall light snapped on, the bedroom door flew open, and his older brother, Brett, stood over him bare-chested, his boxer shorts twisted.

Turned out he was screaming for real.

"Hey, shut up!" Brett hissed. "You're going to wake up Dad."

Kendall tried to push back the blankets. He couldn't feel his legs, and he fought the panic rising in his chest. "Why can't I wake Dad up?"

"He just got to bed an hour ago."

"What time is it?"

"Almost two A.M."

Sitting up, Kendall tried to wiggle his toes. They wouldn't budge. He couldn't even tell if they were still attached to his feet.

"He just got back from another big date with Ms. Juanita Lovato. Looks like you're going to get a new mother."

"So are you."

"Not me. Pretty soon I'll be long gone, get my own place or something."

Or something, Kendall thought.

Brett lay back on the bed and stared up at the ceiling. "So what were you dreaming?"

Kendall didn't speak at first. He felt stupid saying it out loud. Perspiration rolled down his armpits. "Brett, I can't move my legs. They're not there anymore."

"What are you talking about? Your foot's poking me in the shoulder right now."

Taking a deep breath, Kendall forced his knees to bend. Miraculously, they slid upward and formed a mountain under the blanket. His toes began to tingle painfully.

Brett pushed at Kendall's legs. "See, they're here, they work just fine."

"I dreamed my legs were cut off. My feet, I mean."

Brett adjusted the pillow. "You mean amputated?"

"I don't know . . . I couldn't run anymore."

Kendall couldn't imagine anything worse than not being able to run. He ran like other people breathed. Generations of Snake Clan runners had passed their power on to him. Their blood was in his veins. The fact that he was the last living Snake Runner just made the power stronger.

"You've been having spooky dreams since you got back. Ever since they initiated you."

Kendall looked at his brother. "Without my feet, I never ran again." That freaked him out. What made him say that? He was talking in the past tense, like something had already happened.

"Man, look at my arms. You're giving me the shivers."

The trailer house creaked in the night. Kendall heard the wind rise. Something bumped against the window. There were scurrying noises like neighborhood cats chasing mice.

7

Brett rolled over, curious, seeking confidences. "So what happens in the kiva? Was it scary? Did they make you do weird stuff?"

Kendall stared at him. His brother's tousled blond hair and sleep-lined face suddenly bugged him. "Why don't you just get lost?"

"Calm down. I didn't mean anything by it. What's wrong with you? This is the third time you've screamed bloody murder in the middle of the night."

"No way. I did not scream bloody murder."

"You were asleep and don't remember."

"You're lying."

"Don't believe me. But something's going on inside that brain of yours."

Brett tapped Kendall's forehead with his knuckles, then slid off the bed.

Kendall punched the pillow with his fist. His legs felt okay now.

"See, you're fine. All body parts functioning," Brett said from the doorway. "Go back to sleep."

"Shut up."

Brett smiled serenely. "You want some warm milk, honey?"

Kendall jumped off the bed, grabbed one of his Nikes from the floor, and threw it.

Laughing softly, his brother ducked and closed the door. The sneaker hit the wall, knocking a picture of his mother onto the floor. The glass broke, cracking right down the middle of her face.

Kendall climbed back into bed and held the broken picture on top of his chest, hoping he could stay awake the rest of the night. He didn't want to sink back into the hole that had swallowed him a month ago. He hadn't told anybody about it. Not even the medicine man. He touched his arm where the fire had burned him. A tiny scar was there, a circular red spot where the skin hadn't completely healed yet. Only Kendall knew the scar existed. Sometimes he touched it as proof that he hadn't dreamed what had happened that night.

Kendall knew that visions were possible. But when the kiva floor had fallen away, he'd gone to a place where it felt like days had passed. Not a different place, but a different time. A time when evil and fear ruled the desert pueblo. A time when fear was real.

CHAPTER
TWO

The sheets clung in sweaty knots around Kendall's legs in the morning, and his mother's picture had dropped to the floor. He picked it up and set it on the dresser, wondering if Dad would take him to buy a new frame.

In the bathroom he peed and threw on a T-shirt and some shorts, then jogged outside to run his morning miles.

School would be starting in a couple of weeks—ninth grade—and this year he would be one of the younger boys on the cross-country team. Long distances were his specialty ever since he'd run all those miles across the Acoma desert to find Armando at the sacred shrine.

The powerful spirits of the ancient Snake Runners stayed with him, even when he was back home with Dad and Brett in the real world. *Real world!* As if the village of Sky City, sitting on top of its four-hundred-foot mesa, weren't real. The desert, the wild horses, the sacred Enchanted Mesa rising like an island in the middle of scrub and rocks—it was the most real place he'd ever been. And yet, things that were not of this world happened there.

Kendall picked up his pace as he ran along the narrow, dusty paths near the river. Sand crunched under his toes. Flat brown water could be seen through miles of dense cottonwood trees growing close against the banks. Morning sunlight sparkled. The day was heating up already, but the giant trees kept things cool and shady. The river was a private place to run. A place to feel the elusive power of the Snake Clan runners flow through his body. He could feel the magic tugging at his legs, his feet, and especially his heart.

Kendall ducked under a low-hanging branch and skirted a fallen log. Even though it had been only a month since the initiation, he already missed Acoma, the quiet village sitting close to the clouds. Running also made him miss his great-grandfather Armando. Kendall wished he could go back in time, before Armando got hurt on his last run to the sacred shrine. Before Armando was gone forever.

He would have asked more questions, tried to learn more about the runners and his lost clan. He would also have asked more about his mother's life growing up at Acoma with her grandparents. Armando had become her father when her own had died in Korea.

Circling back around to the ditch banks, Kendall finally headed home. When the mobile home came into view, Kendall sprinted, tearing around the final corner. At the front yard, he stopped and grabbed the chain-link fence.

Dad's glossy red eighteen-wheeler rumbled in the driveway. The engine hood slammed shut, and Dad shoved his tool case into the back of the cab.

"Hey," he called as Kendall entered the gate.

"Hey," Kendall said, wondering what was up. Dad had shaved so smooth that not a trace of his reddish stubble showed. His shirt was pressed, jeans brand-new, hands grease-free.

"I've got an overnight haul to Kingman," Dad said.

"Since when?"

"Since . . . I already told you about it."

Kendall shook his head. "No, you didn't."

Dad reached inside for his log. "I must've told Brett and thought I told you, too."

"Can I go with you?"

His father looked startled by the question. "Sorry, Kendall, but I'm afraid not. I promised Juanita I'd take her. She's never had a trip in a semi before."

His father's words were so unexpected, Kendall almost fell over. Since when had Dad and Juanita started doing weekend stuff or overnighters? He felt his mouth turn sour, and his heart began to thump.

"This is her last free week," Dad said. "They're moving her room at the high school, and she's gotta set up before registration. So I, uh, invited her, you know." Dad looked away and flipped out a pen, jotting notes in his truck logbook.

The patchy grass spun in front of Kendall's eyes. He pushed through the front door, wishing his thoughts would slow down so he could make sense of what was happening.

Dad came through the front door behind him. "I'm ready to take off."

"Can Brett take me to Acoma for the weekend?"

"No." The answer came quickly, harshly. Dad picked up his shaving bag. "You spent most of the summer there. I want you to stay home now until next summer."

"Dad—"

"Maybe Christmas break for a short visit," his father amended.

"If you're not going to be home anyway, what does it matter?"

"I don't think it's appropriate for you to be out there so much. Especially with your mother and great-grandfather gone."

"But I have a place to stay at Armando's old house, the Snake Clan home. And Cousin Trina—"

"I said no."

The abrupt silence was full of unspoken words. Kendall felt tears sting his eyelids. That made him feel stupid. He didn't want to cry about this.

Dad turned and walked out the front door, clicking it softly behind him. Kendall sank to the kitchen floor, fighting the quiver in his jaw as he leaned against the doorframe, elbows on his knees. He put a hand over his eyes. Everything was happening too fast. Mom had been so beautiful, always carrying a soft, knowing smile and kind dark eyes. Juanita Lovato was a pale shadow in comparison. His father seemed to have forgotten so fast.

Across the room, Brett turned on the television. "I think Dad's hiding something."

"*Shut up!*" Kendall said. He didn't want to think about it.

Dad should have come back inside. He should have said a proper goodbye. Instead, he hurried off to meet Juanita.

Mrs. Weigert, their elderly neighbor, called Juanita the "new lady" in Dad's life. He had met her at Brett's high school graduation. Why did she have to be a teacher, like their mother? At least she didn't teach English and creative writing like Mom had. Ms. Lovato taught history, "with an emphasis on New Mexico," as she put it one night when Dad brought her home for dinner.

She was younger than Mom, too. That night, Kendall

13

had asked Juanita how old she was right at the dinner table. He didn't know what made him do that. Asking her age was something a little kid would have done. It was just so strange to have a woman sitting in Mom's spot, smiling and touching Dad's arm when she spoke.

His father was mortified, shooting daggers at Kendall with his eyes.

Juanita gave a little laugh, glancing around the table.

Brett kept eating, but under the table Kendall felt a sharp kick right in the shin. Kendall tried to kick his brother back, but Brett moved away too fast, grinning the whole time and shoveling food into his mouth.

"I'm thirty-four, Kendall," she answered.

Dad grounded Kendall the next day. Kept him home and wouldn't let him out even to run. Kendall had to wash the entire rig. By himself. No TV either. And he had to fix dinner for everyone, even her. He made the mutton stew recipe his great-grandfather had taught him, hoping she would gag.

Kendall studied her as she carefully chewed her stew. She even swallowed the tough meat, not trying to hide it in her napkin like a lot of people did. Juanita was pretty, he supposed, but nothing like his mother. In a way Kendall was glad, and in a way he wasn't, which he knew didn't make a bit of sense.

Juanita's hair was dark brown and short, styled like a business executive's, not like Mom's long black hair. Those first evenings Dad brought her over, she wore crisp linen suits with heels, completely different from Mom's flowing skirts. Juanita also had big, perfect white teeth and talked a lot. Mom's soft-spoken voice had always been calm and soothing and she didn't chatter near as much.

Dad defended her, of course. "You guys make her nervous the way you keep staring at her, waiting for her to choke on her food or break a plate."

Soon Dad was calling her Nita and putting his arm around her as they watched a rented video. Kendall didn't call her anything. He didn't even want to look at her, but his own eyes betrayed him. He constantly stole glances to see what she was doing. He wanted to know what she was saying, if she was touching Dad, if Dad was touching her.

The next Saturday night, Dad ordered Chinese take-out and brought her home again, putting on an old Beatles record.

They were talking about New Mexico history, her "passion," as Juanita called it. "Think about what this state would be like if the Spaniards hadn't come this direction," she was saying as Kendall ate the last egg roll. "The whole Southwest, in fact. The culture, the traditions, the food we eat, our expressions. I still speak Spanish with my parents."

Dad leaned back in his chair, listening intently. "Every part of the country has its own unique style because of the people who settled it. Interesting to think about."

"I even have an ancestor from the sixteenth century who was part of Juan de Oñate's group."

Dad gave a low whistle. "Your family has been here a long time."

"My grandfather used to tell me incredible stories about their travels. Like Oñate, most explorers came north through Mexico. Thousands of miles over deserts, cutting their own trails, settling the land, even dying along the way. I read some old journals and got hooked. I guess it's not a surprise I ended up a history teacher."

"To be part of Oñate's expedition must have really been something," Dad told her. "They recently put up a statue or something to him, didn't they?"

Kendall put down his fork. He'd heard of Oñate and the early conquistadors from his cousin Trina at Acoma. Trina could tell the story like nobody else could. Kendall picked at his food while Juanita kept talking. He was trying to remember the details, but he hadn't ever learned the whole story. Something about a battle on top of Acoma. Blood staining the rocks.

Kendall's attention swung back to the table again as he heard Juanita say, "They made a beautiful place out of empty, desolate land."

Kendall couldn't stop himself from arguing with her. "Empty land? There were lots of people already living here."

Juanita gave an embarrassed laugh. "Of course there were, but the lifestyle of the native tribes, and even their religion, was primitive in comparison. The Europeans brought a more advanced culture and civilization, which helped everyone. They also believed it was their destiny to come settle this exciting new world and convert the native people."

He couldn't help challenging her. "I've heard about the wars with the conquistadors. Some tribes were wiped out. A lot of people got killed."

Juanita tried to smile at him, but Kendall just stared back. "Yes, there was some bloodshed. On both sides. There usually is when two different groups want to live in the same place. But many of the stories have been exaggerated."

Kendall closed his eyes. She always seemed to twist everything around. "May I be excused?"

"I think that's a good idea," Dad said, trying to give him disapproving look, but Kendall wouldn't meet his eye.

Kendall pushed back his chair and set his dinner plate in the sink with a crash. How did Juanita know what people wanted or how they felt? Especially people four hundred years ago. As if she knew what was best.

When Kendall left the room, his father and Juanita glanced at him in unison. Their fluid, mirroring motion was almost spooky. As if they were already *together*.

Whenever Kendall looked at her, he got the strangest feeling he was looking at his oldest enemy. He tried to shake it off.

After dinner Kendall had kitchen duty. Instead of paper plates, they'd used Mom's good dishes. They only did that for company. Or people Dad wanted to impress. Kendall slowly filled the sink with water and squirted in a glob of dish soap.

Suddenly, Juanita was beside him, hovering near his shoulder. He could smell her perfume.

"Hey, you want some help?"

Kendall felt himself stiffen. "Don't need any help."

"I'll just rinse and dry, then." She found a towel and began to stack the dirty dishes for him.

It looked like she was determined not to go away. Why was she hanging around him? Especially after the history lesson at dinner.

"Where's Dad?" he asked.

"Out tinkering on the rig with Brett. Those two are a lot like, aren't they?"

"I guess so." Whatever that was supposed to mean.

Kendall stuck a soapy glass under the hot water. Juani[ta] took it from him and laid it upside down on the drying rac[k].

"I have a feeling you must look a lot like your mother.'

Kendall grabbed another plate. Man, she was brilliant.

Kendall washed in silence, and Juanita seemed to co[n]centrate on rinsing everything until it was squeaky clean.

Juanita cleared her throat. "Kendall, I'm sorry if I [of]fended you at dinner tonight."

He just shrugged. He didn't want to give her any sati[s]faction. He had a thousand things he wished he could say [or] do, but they had to stay bottled up inside. Sometimes it fe[lt] like he would explode. Juanita didn't belong here in th[e] kitchen. He wished she would go away and leave him [to] work by himself. Doing the dishes together felt like so[me] kind of mother-and-son chore, and he didn't like it. But [he] knew he couldn't be rude, either. Dad would ground him f[or] a month.

"Do these plates go in this cupboard?" Juanita asked.

"Yeah." One-syllable words. That was good.

Juanita shut the cupboard and started drying the glasse[s]. "You've probably figured out that I'm a pretty direct perso[n]. And I know that I'm very different from your mother. [Of] course, I'm not trying to be your mother or replace her. [I] would never do that."

Kendall froze in his spot, wishing she would stop. Ju[st] shut up, he thought.

"Your father has told me about her, and she sounds like [a] wonderful person."

For some reason just hearing that really got Kendal[l]

blood boiling. He didn't want Dad talking to Juanita about Mom. Discussing her. He hated the thought of him doing that. He had no right, and he should have told Kendall before he started sharing private family stuff. Now Kendall wondered what Dad had talked about, what kind of details.

If Mom hadn't died, they wouldn't be discussing her at all. Juanita wouldn't be here. She wouldn't even exist. That's how it was supposed to be. Kendall stared at the dissolving suds and felt a fork jabbing his thumb from the bottom of the sink. He pressed harder, trying to make it hurt.

Juanita quietly added, "I'm sure you miss her a lot."

Kendall turned to her. "Just shut up, will you? You don't know anything!"

He heard her take a quick breath. He'd shocked her. He was glad, but it didn't make him feel any better.

Juanita sighed. "I'm not very good at this, and I'm really sorry, Kendall." He heard her voice tremble ever so slightly. "Your father is one of the best men I've ever known, and I care about him a great deal."

Kendall didn't respond, just chewed on his lip and unplugged the drain, listening to the gurgling sound of the water as it was sucked down the pipe.

Juanita finished the glasses and carefully arranged them in the overhead cabinet. "I don't know if it will make any difference to you, but I do know a little bit about how you feel."

Kendall wondered how she could possibly know what it felt like to lose your mother.

"Has your father told you much about me?" she asked suddenly.

Kendall shrugged again. "Nope."

"Oh." She said it like she was surprised that Kendall's dad hadn't talked about her at all. Like she was hoping he had. Maybe Dad *had* talked about her, but when it came to Juanita, Kendall never paid any attention.

"I lost someone, too. Many years ago. I had a son, a little boy. He died of leukemia when he was four years old."

Kendall didn't know what he was supposed to say to that. Did she want him to feel sorry for her? It struck him that both his mom and Juanita's son had died of cancer. Was that supposed to make things better between them?

Kendall dried his hands and slammed the towel drawer. He turned to leave the kitchen. He felt like stalking off, but something made him stop. He raised his head. Juanita was blinking her eyes a lot, like she was about to cry.

If his dad had known he was being such a jerk, he'd have been in big trouble. But Kendall didn't want to make his father angry; he just wanted his dad back again. Since Mom was gone, they'd grown closer, and Dad had always been easy to talk to. He'd always been the kind of dad that hugged him. He even cried over stuff, especially when he talked about Mom. Kendall had always liked that for some reason. It gave him a secure feeling. But lately, his father hadn't talked about her at all.

Kendall realized he'd been standing there looking at Juanita for several moments. She was still at the silverware drawer, staring back at him, waiting. Now he felt like an idiot.

"Sorry," he muttered, hoping she knew he meant he was sorry about her child. Then he hurried out the door.

Kendall hoped she wasn't trying to replace her son. He knew that was a stupid thing to think, and he knew deep down she wasn't doing that. But then again, he wasn't volunteering for the job.

CHAPTER
THREE

All weekend Kendall tried not to think about Dad trucking across Arizona with Juanita. Tried not to think about what they were doing, where they stopped to eat, what they talked about. Where they stopped to sleep.

Sunday night Brett brought home Burger King, spilling bags of food over the countertop. They ate at the kitchen table, music cranked up on the stereo, but Kendall couldn't stop watching the clock.

He was getting up to find the ketchup when suddenly his dad and Juanita were standing in the kitchen doorway, arms around each other, like they'd just come back from a drive around the block instead of an entire state away.

Dad was grinning, although he looked like he was trying to suppress it. He was even wearing a clean shirt tucked into his Levi's. Must not have been any leaky oil problems.

Dad yelled over the music. "Hey, it's late for dinner, isn't it?"

Kendall watched the two adults together, appraising them.

"Good trip?" Brett asked.

Kendall looked away, not wanting to see the confirmation in his father's face.

"Truck ran great. Good gas mileage, too."

"Hello, Kendall," Juanita said.

Kendall grunted, his glance sliding across his father's

22

ace and away. He didn't return to his seat. He'd have to brush past her. He opened the refrigerator and pretended to look for mustard.

"As soon as you guys finish eating," Dad said, "we'd like to talk to you."

Slamming the refrigerator, Kendall picked up his soda and started down the hall.

"Not so fast," Dad said lightly, reaching for his arm but missing.

"Can't a person use the bathroom?" Kendall said as he slammed the door.

He stalled, looking at his face in the mirror. A tiny zit was starting at his hairline. Opening a tube of benzoyl peroxide, he rubbed on a glob. Then he loosened the leather tie holding his hair back and let the length of blackness fall below his shoulders. He brushed his hair back off his face with his fingers. It felt just like Mom's hair used to when she bent over to kiss him good night.

Kendall let his face go blank. That was good. He looked tough, aloof. Past feeling.

Brett knocked. "You fall in?"

Kendall threw open the door.

"You forgot to flush," Brett said.

"I didn't go."

His brother threw up his hands. "Dad wants us in the living room."

Kendall blinked and hit the door with his fist.

Brett added, "You know they're going to tell us they want to get mar—"

"Don't say it!"

"Maybe they just want to move in together first. They could end up hating each other after a few months and then it would all be over," Brett said cheerfully.

It sounded good, but Kendall didn't like it when people lived together. It just didn't feel right to him. How could love be an experiment? It either was or it wasn't. You got married and made it last forever. But he didn't want his dad marrying Juanita. He wanted his father to stay true to Mom forever. He knew it didn't make sense, but he didn't need a new mother—why did Dad need a new wife?

"All you gotta do is hang on," Brett went on. "Ignore her for six months, and everything will go back to normal, okay?"

"You have weird logic," Kendall told him. But maybe his brother had a point. In a few months this could all be over. But what if it wasn't? Dad wasn't the kind of person to hook up with lots of girlfriends. Juanita was the first woman he'd really dated since Mom's death.

Juanita and his father were whispering on the couch. Dad leaned over and kissed her—a long one. Kendall watched, unable to pull his eyes away.

She looked up, smiling. Radiant. That was the word. But why would she be so radiant? His stomach started to hurt. Too many hamburgers.

Juanita also seemed more relaxed than usual. She wasn't trying to make a good impression any longer. Maybe it was the faded blue jeans and white embroidered blouse.

"Hey, buddy," Dad murmured. "How was your weekend?"

"Okay." He shook his hair back and stared at him.

"I didn't realize your hair was past your shoulders, Kendall," Juanita said. "How long did it take to grow?"

24

Kendall shrugged. "Few months."

"Sit down, Kendall, sit down," Dad laughed. "You're making me nervous."

"I'd rather stand."

He knew he was making this hard for his dad, but why should he give him a break? His father hadn't consulted him or asked his feelings. His dad used to talk about everything. He never kept things secret. Until Juanita Lovato.

"We know what's going on, so just get it over with and let me go to bed, will you?"

His father dropped his hand from Juanita's clasp. "How could you possibly know already?"

Juanita gave a nervous laugh and looked at Kendall's dad. Something happened in her face, and she tried to convey a message in a flicker of a second, but Dad didn't get it.

Kendall flexed his fists. It seemed to take all his strength to stand there. Waiting for the bomb to drop.

Dad glanced around the room, puzzled. "Who told you guys we got married this weekend? We haven't even talked to anyone else yet."

Brett fell off his chair. He started laughing, then he started coughing.

Dad jumped up, his face stern. "I didn't know it was so funny."

Juanita murmured, "I don't think Brett thinks it's funny."

Kendall's pulse pounded in his head. It moved down into his chest. He could even feel it in his bones. He suddenly realized that Juanita was staring at him. Almost as if she knew his thoughts. He wanted her to disappear. He wanted them all to just go away. This couldn't be happening. Dad was supposed to say they were engaged. Not the other. Not this.

"Kingman's only an hour from Las Vegas. Didn't even need a judge," Dad said.

"We thought it would be easier for everyone," Juanita spoke up. "No wedding reception, invitations, guests, all the fuss . . ." Her voice trailed off.

"It was spur-of-the-moment," Dad added, and his voice betrayed excitement he couldn't contain. "Last night actually."

Dad grinned then, and before he could stop himself, Kendall lunged forward, barreling into his father's stomach and knocking him off his feet. He felt like a little kid, mad at his dad, stomping his feet, but he couldn't help it.

Behind him, Juanita cried out as the couch broke his father's fall. Kendall felt Brett's hands reaching for him, but he slipped out of his brother's grasp.

"Kendall!" Brett said, sounding shocked. "What are you, a maniac?"

Kendall ignored them all. In three leaps, he was out the front door, disappearing into the night.

He ran until he felt like he was underwater. He was going to drown. He was already drowning. Dad and Juanita Lovato had eloped. The thought was unreal. *Married*. To *her*.

Lights pierced the forest of cottonwood trees lining the riverbanks. Those were Dad's Taurus headlights. The engine rattled softly across the night air. They'd never find him. He could run where cars couldn't drive.

Kendall kept moving, legs pumping, feet pounding. A few minutes later, he reached the edge of the cemetery. He jumped the sagging wooden fence. Tufts of grass were trying to grow through the soft sand in the newer part of the cemetery, and most of the headstones were still above ground. He never went to the old cemetery section built near the arroyo. Nobody did. It was a maze of graves two hundred years old with tombstones that had sunk right down into the earth. It was also a patchwork of holes. Underground holes that made up an entire village of rattlesnake nests.

Racing over the rise, three rows across and five headstones down, Kendall finally stopped, dropping in front of a pearly white slab. An orange streetlight helped him see the outline of the letters, even though he couldn't read them in the dark. He traced his mother's name with his fingers. *Rebecca Abeyta Drennan, Beloved Wife and Mother*.

He came here by himself sometimes, but not very often. He knew his mother wasn't here. She lived at Acoma, among the spirits that roamed the valley. He had found her there on that night after his long journey across the desert to rescue his great-grandfather at the sacred shrine. The vision would always stay with him: her face, her voice, her long hair blowing against a black sky of raindrops.

A breeze lifted his own sweaty hair, and Kendall hunched over, willing her to talk to him. Only the silence of the summer night spoke back. How could he go home, knowing his father and Juanita were in his parents' room—together?

He crouched there, breathing hard, shaking from running so fast, suddenly cold. Then Kendall felt a presence. He heard a noise. Something tinkled softly to his right. A gentle rattling, like stones in the bottom of a metal can. Very slowly, he turned his head.

Behind his mother's grave site, a rattlesnake raised its

head. The reptile slithered closer, wrapping its body around the headstone, crushing a bouquet of wilted chrysanthemums blown in by the wind.

He kept his eyes on the snake's face just like his great-grandfather had taught him. Kendall mapped out an escape route in his head. The rattlesnake coiled its body, and its tongue tasted the air. Tasted him.

Every muscle in Kendall's body was taut, alert.

He slowly hissed at the reptile. "I am Snake Clan."

The snake just stared at him with beady black eyes.

The next moment, Kendall leaped to his feet and vaulted over the headstone behind him. He ran down the hill, tore through tumbleweeds, and headed for home. He knew what he was going to do now. It was easy. The rattlesnake was his sign.

Kendall sneaked into the house and quietly made it to his room. He pulled his gym bag out of the closet and stuffed underwear, shorts, and a couple of T-shirts inside. On top of the clothes he laid his leather girdle and water pouch, the embroidered sash and handmade moccasins his great-grandfather had given him.

He crept down the hall so his dad and Juanita wouldn't hear him. After washing the sweat off his face in the bathroom, he tied his long hair back with a leather strap.

His brother lay spread-eagle on top of the sheets in his room. The August night was warm, and the window was wide open.

Kendall tapped Brett on the arm, and his brother jerked awake.

"Shh!" Kendall hissed.

"Who's that—my maniac brother?"

"I need your help," Kendall whispered.

"Go away. I'm having a good dream about Sarah."

"You can finish it later."

Brett's head thumped back onto his pillow. "She says she won't wait."

Kendall crouched on the floor. "Get up."

"In the middle of the night?"

"Morning is too late."

Brett's eyelids rose again. "What are you talking about?" Leaning on one elbow, he added, "By the way, where the hell did you go? You scared everybody, even Juanita."

"I don't care about her."

Brett grinned. "You sure do hide well."

Kendall smiled back. "Easy when it's dark and you know every running path in the county."

Brett gave a short laugh.

"I want you to drive me out to Acoma."

"You have now crossed the border of insanity," Brett said loudly.

"Shh! You're going to wake them up!"

"They're not here. Dad went to Juanita's place."

Kendall shot him a look. He hadn't expected that.

"I dropped them off since I need the car for work tomorrow. Juanita thought you needed a day to get used to the idea before she spent the night here."

"You mean before she moved in."

"Yeah, and I promised Dad I'd wait up for you."

"You broke your promise."

"I heard you come in, then I fell asleep. But you know, it's their honeymoon."

"Quit saying stuff like that, will you?"

29

"Okay. I'm sorry. Really, I am."

"We can drive over there now, and you'll be back before it's time to go to work."

"You can't run away from this, Kendall."

"After what Dad pulled, he can't stop me."

They stared at each other in silence; then Brett sighed.

"Man, you owe me for this. Big-time."

Kendall closed his eyes with relief. For the moment, for a little while, he was free. He was going to Acoma.

Brett pulled on a pair of Levi's, then jammed a baseball cap onto his head. He grabbed the Taurus keys and his wallet. "If we're going, let's go."

Clutching his bag, Kendall stole past the eighteen-wheeler as if someone might be sitting in the cab spying through the windshield.

When Brett started the ignition, the car coughed softly. He put it in first gear, released the brake, and rolled down the driveway. Fifteen minutes later, they were on the highway, heading west. They didn't pass a single car for miles; then a few semis roared past. It seemed to take hours to get there, but Kendall was surprised when the exit suddenly appeared in front of them.

Moonlight washed the road. Clumps of scrub bordered the soft shoulder of the highway. Flat, low mesas loomed in the distance, silhouetted against a crystalline black sky.

"This is crazy," Brett said. "Dad would kill us if he knew what we were doing. I take that back—Dad will kill me when I get home. What am I gonna tell him?"

"The truth."

"Which would be . . . ?"

"You know as well as I do."

Brett nodded gravely. "I do, I do."

Everything seemed packed with meaning.

"I'll tell him it's fourteen-year-old hormones."

Kendall punched him and Brett laughed, raising an arm to defend himself.

"Hey," Brett said. "Coming here is only temporary, you know."

Kendall nodded, then held up a hand. "This is it."

The headlights cut the blackness like a spotlight. There were no streetlights out here on Acoma land.

Brett jammed on the brakes. "How can you tell?"

"Nighttime in the desert is my specialty."

Brett rolled off the asphalt and parked on the dirt. The silence was sudden and immense, just like the view of the desert on the other side of the windshield. Endless, dark, and silent.

Brett glanced across the seat. "I can't figure you out. I guess you needed Mom more than me. You look just like her. You talk like her. The things you say . . . like 'nighttime in the desert,' stuff like that. Did you know she used to write when Dad was gone on long hauls?"

Kendall nodded, then realized Brett probably couldn't see him.

"I can't believe it's been three years already," Brett went on. "That first year was so hard every day felt like a month."

"I know," Kendall said. Sometimes the nights felt even longer. That was the time he and Mom had always talked in his bedroom before he went to sleep. The times she told him stories of Acoma and he listened to her voice speaking softly in the dark, felt her hand smoothing his hair back from his face.

31

"You seemed like such a little kid when she got sick, but you remember, don't you?"

He and Brett had never talked about Mom like this before. The atmosphere inside the car was close, intense.

"I know her still. Sometimes, I can hear her voice." Kendall paused. "Two years ago I saw her. At Enchanted Mesa. She was there."

Kendall could feel his brother's eyes on him. "You really saw her? How? You mean like a vision?"

"Something like that, but I don't want to talk about it right now."

Brett sighed. "I'm getting the creeps sitting here in the dark. I can't even see the village."

"There's no electricity, and Sky City is still three miles up ahead. We're right across from Enchanted Mesa."

Brett peered out his window. The yellow moon had disappeared behind a cloud. "Let me take you to the village."

"This is where I want to be. Enchanted Mesa will tell me what to do."

"Now you're talking crazy again. Tell me about it. I really want to know. Is it that private?"

Kendall shrugged. "Just hard to explain." He opened the car door and the dome light came on. Brett's face looked pale and tired. Kendall grabbed his gym bag, looped it over his shoulder, and slammed the door. He came around to the driver's side as Brett rolled down his window.

"Kendall." Brett's voice sounded tight. "I don't have a good feeling about this—"

Kendall put his hand on the window ledge. "This is my home. I can figure things out here."

Kendall turned to leave and Brett stopped him.

"Wait a minute. You know those dreams? What happened at the kiva? You don't scream in the middle of the night for nothing."

Kendall grinned. "It's top-secret. If I told you, I'd have to kill you."

Brett rolled his eyes. "Smart-ass." He reached out and grabbed Kendall's arm. Their eyes locked. "I'm coming back for you in three days. Earlier maybe—depends how mad Dad is. Don't be surprised if he storms in here later today."

"He won't be coming." Kendall's throat closed up. "He's on his honeymoon, remember?"

"Don't think about it. Go run. Run fifty miles if you have to, but get your head together. I'll give you three days. Max."

"See you," Kendall said, then hefted his bag and walked into the darkness.

He heard Brett start up the engine and slowly pull away, gravel crunching like glass shards on a kitchen floor.

Kendall kept walking. The desert was quiet. Here it was only sand, scrub grass, and small stones, as familiar as his own backyard. He reached the monstrous boulders at the base of the sacred mesa in about ten minutes.

Across the flat valley, the village of Sky City, on its ancient rock citadel, was dark. Not even kerosene lanterns lit up any of the small square windows. It was probably about four-thirty in the morning, and everyone was asleep.

Setting his bag down, Kendall stripped, folding his clothes into the bottom of the bag. One by one, he put on the Snake Runner garments. His leather breechcloth went on first. Then he picked up the sacred bundle Armando had given him the last summer he was alive. Kendall opened it for just a moment, fingering the tiny sacred ear of white corn from their first mother, *Iatuk*, who came from *Sipapu*, the place of emergence. Also in the bag was his miniature prayer stick tied with eagle feathers, a sack of herbs, and last of all, the carved snake. He tied the bundle to his waist with a sash, then slipped on the turquoise necklace Armando had crafted for him.

Putting on his Snake Clan garments under a sky filled with stars made his eyes sting with tears. He would always remember the night he stood on top of the flat roof of the house and Armando dressed him in his Snake Runner clothes for the first time. That was the night Kendall had become a Snake Runner, too.

The last thing he tied to his waist was Armando's old leather water pouch. Kendall was glad he'd filled it in the kitchen before leaving home. He loosened his long hair out of its leather clasp, feeling it fall across his bare shoulders.

Stashing his bag behind a wedge of rocks, Kendall surveyed the land under the drifting moonlight. He felt the ancient cords of magic pulling him south to the miniature replica of Enchanted Mesa. He could see it glowing under the starlight. The dreams pulled him there. It was time to find out why.

Slowly, Kendall took off running. The magic of the valley enveloped him, and he raced toward it.

Running from home. Running to answers.

Straight into his nightmares.

CHAPTER
FOUR

There was enough moonlight to run by. Kendall skirted tall, spindly cholla cacti and clusters of prickly pear. An owl hooted overhead, and wings rushed through the air above him. It wasn't long before Kendall was in his rhythm. He had left his shoes inside his gym bag, so he was barefoot, but it didn't bother him. Barefoot was how he was meant to run at Acoma. And he was used to it after the summer. The ground felt warm, rough rocks only a minor nuisance.

He passed Enchanted Mesa on the edge of the narrow highway, leaving behind what he knew best. Settling into an easy run, Kendall moved past clumps of scrub and rocks as he focused on the miniature mesa five miles to the south. He could already see its white walls glowing faintly up ahead. He hadn't gone near the little mesa since he'd come this way to find Armando at the sacred shrine. The power around this replica of Enchanted Mesa was so strong it was almost frightening.

He couldn't understand why it would call to him. The strength it evoked was unnerving, yet magnetic. He had asked the elders once if it had magical powers from the gods, but they were puzzled by his questions.

"Perhaps only you feel its spirit," one of the men had suggested. "Perhaps there is something there for you and your clan."

When the elder said those words, Kendall knew the power he felt must be because of the Snake Clan, his clan. And he was now the only person who could find out.

The sculpted mesa with its rose-colored sheer walls must hold answers about the clan, information about the past. The thought made Kendall run faster. His great-grandfather had died before he was able to tell Kendall the history and roots to the magic. No one else knew them any longer. Those sacred things had died suddenly with Armando Abeyta.

And yet the dreams told him that something horrible waited for him. Would he be able to face it? He wouldn't know until he found it.

Reaching into his waistband, Kendall pulled out the tiny prayer stick he had finished carving before leaving Acoma a month ago. It was the best one he'd ever made, sanded to feel like satin in his palm and adorned with delicate white turkey feathers.

Kendall slowed for a moment, whipping his head around. He could have sworn he'd just heard footsteps following him. Felt the earth tremble with faint vibrations. Blackness swirled everywhere, like a bottle of ink had been poured across the valley floor. Then Kendall heard heavy breathing behind his left shoulder. Spooked, he whirled around in the dark.

The ghost of an ancient runner flew past, sinewy legs pumping, black hair flying.

"Hey!" Kendall yelled, barely missing a cedar bush sitting directly in his path.

The runner disappeared into the night.

There was a rushing of spirits on every side. Kendall felt

chills crawl up and down his arms, and then he stopped dead in his tracks.

An elderly man ran right by him, long white hair blowing in an invisible breeze. Kendall felt the old man's arm brush his shoulder as he passed. Like the whisper of the wind.

Kendall's heart began to pound. "Grandfather!" he called, and his own voice shook in the stillness. The runner's footsteps faded away into the silence. Kendall started to sprint again, trying to follow, but the spirits had gone.

An owl hooted overhead, wings beating the air.

Kendall took a deep breath. Sweat poured off him, even though the night air was cool. When he reached the perimeter of the towering miniature rock mesa, he sucked in the strong sensations and was nearly knocked over. The spirits of the ancients, the magic, was truly immense.

Kendall tried to keep his wits about him. The mesa sparkled under the fading stars as dawn approached. Running swiftly, Kendall threw back his head to see the peak kissing the sky two hundred feet in the air. It was beautiful. Red and purple rock blended together like a ribbon had wound itself around the golden walls.

As he got closer, he noticed a crevice on the west, a fissure like an opening in the rock. Kendall climbed over the boulders sitting in his path, then through piles of rocky shale lying at the base. When he reached the high, straight walls, he stuck his fingers into a crack at the opening of the crevice and wedged the prayer stick inside.

Closing his eyes, Kendall felt the magic wash over him, filling him until he could hardly breathe. He couldn't delay any longer. It was time to go inside the mesa itself.

The entrance turned pitch-black within a few steps. He

had to feel his way along with his hands and toes. The path felt dry and dusty. Images of rattlers and bottomless pits filled his mind. The walls closed in narrowly as the path sloped upward, winding to the right. Kendall stopped suddenly when his hands touched something.

Lightly rubbing his fingers along the walls, he could feel indentations in the stone. He walked back and forth several feet, trying to make out what they were. Just cracks in the walls or something more? When he stopped to feel more closely, he swore there were figures or words carved right into the smooth stone. He would need to come back when it was daylight. Whether it was graffiti or something else was hard to tell.

Kendall continued walking. The ceiling of rock hung lower and lower. Then a shower of light burst in front of his eyes as he whacked his skull and fell to his knees in pain. He touched his forehead. A small gash trickled blood.

Dizzy now, he got up and stumbled along the corridor. It felt like he'd gone a mile, but that seemed impossible. He wasn't sure of his direction any longer. Finally, a fragment of daylight appeared ahead. The shadowy tunnel swam before his eyes.

Soft footsteps echoed. In the dim recesses the figure of a woman with flowing black hair moved through the narrow corridor in front of him. Kendall started to run after her.

"Mom, wait!"

The apparition stayed just ahead of him no matter how fast he went, a shadow weaving along the rocky path. Suddenly, she turned, smiling gently, beckoning Kendall to follow.

Kendall sped up, nearly touching the hem of her dress before she faded around a bend in the path. All at once Kendall hit the end of the corridor. A blank rock wall. He couldn't believe this was the end. He touched the stone walls, but there was no way out. Frustrated and weary, he wiped at his face, feeling the wet blood.

He had come through the entire mesa, and here he was at the end of the corridor with nothing to show for it. No visions, no sudden knowledge.

He looked up as a sharp light suddenly pierced the crack in the ceiling of rock. It was like watching the sun rise, and Kendall put up a hand to shade his eyes against the brilliance. He dropped to his knees, the light nearly blinding him, and he knew that his mother had led him there. Time seemed to hold its breath, then exhale as the light faded.

Getting up, Kendall began to retrace his steps to the entrance. The dizzy feeling stopped. He touched his brow. The gash was gone. No trace of blood. Something very strange was happening.

Back at the entrance, he stepped out of the narrow crevice. Of course, he had returned to the same place he'd started. There was the crack where he'd placed his prayer stick.

Kendall peered inside to look, then let out a cry. The hole was empty. The prayer stick was gone. Shocked, Kendall took a step backward and tripped on the loose shale. Losing his footing, he pitched down the ten feet of rocky slope to the desert floor, an avalanche of gravel sliding down with him. Stones cut his arms and shoulders as he tried to stop the fall but couldn't.

Landing on his back, Kendall moaned in pain. The impact of the hard ground felt like concrete. He struggled to rise, then gave up and stared at the pink dawn lighting the sky. He waited for the world to stop spinning.

A shadow suddenly loomed over him. Before Kendall could roll away, an Acoma man, barefoot and girdled in a leather breechcloth, shoved a heel onto his chest. Words drowned in Kendall's throat as he lay pinned.

Long black hair framed the stony face of the warrior. Swiftly the young man reared back, pulling an arrow taut through his bow. He let out a shrill war cry, then carefully placed the tip of the sharp arrow at Kendall's throat.

CHAPTER FIVE

Kendall didn't dare move. The young Acoma man's finger held steady, but his eyes narrowed as he surveyed Kendall's leather apron and the sacred bundle secured at his waist.

Kendall saw his moment of confusion, but the man was obviously trained in warfare. The warrior pulled his arm tight and made to release the arrow in sudden, sure death.

"Don't. Please," Kendall pleaded in hoarse Keresan.

The warrior's hand wavered. "Who are you, and how do you know my language?"

"I'm Acoman," Kendall rasped, wincing as the arrow pressed harder against his neck.

"I've never seen you before." He shook his head to deny Kendall's claim, but the arrow retreated an inch.

Kendall wanted to say the same thing. Where did this guy come from? He'd never seen him at the ceremony dances or in the kiva. He looked different, too, in small, subtle ways. His skin was more weathered and sun-darkened than any he'd ever seen, the inflections in his accent and phrasing more pronounced than any he had heard. The man's clothing was obviously hand-sewn; Kendall could see the uneven stitches made with coarse thread.

The way the young man stood gave Kendall the most apprehension. Fearless, so comfortable with his bow and arrow. Too comfortable.

His bow and arrow. Kendall went cross-eyed looking at the primitive weapon. The bow had been carved out of piñon and sanded by hand. In the pouch slung over his shoulder, arrowheads, hand-chiseled from stone, had been tied with leather to each straight wooden arrow.

Kendall knew that something was terribly wrong. Sweat poured down his face as he tried to hold still underneath the arrow poised to kill him and the man's bold scrutiny.

"Where did you come from?" the Acoma warrior demanded.

Kendall's gaze flickered to the flat mesa he'd just crawled through. The miniature Enchanted Mesa was enchanted all right. The passageway had brought him to a different time—Kendall was sure of it. Everything looked the same— the valley, the mesa, the village on top of Sky City to the north, but this man was not from the same time Kendall was. He thought about the blinding light in the corridor, as well as the odd sensation that time was changing around him, and he felt himself trembling.

"Tell me where you have come from," the young man asked again.

"Been away," Kendall managed to say, and his voice cracked, ending in an embarrassing squeak.

The man shook his head. "You look like an Acoman, you speak like an Acoman, but I do not know you. I shall kill you now."

Kendall screamed, "No!" and tried to grab the arrow.

The warrior laughed, keeping his foot on Kendall's chest. "You are no more than a babe. Perhaps I will wait to kill you." Slowly, he withdrew the arrow and placed it in the quiver slung over his back.

When Kendall tried to sit up, the young man forced him back down. He examined Kendall's deerskin water pouch, the sacred bundle at his waist, then finally ran his rough hands over Kendall's muscular legs and callused bare feet.

Their eyes locked. The young man's eyes looked like black marbles. They reflected nothing. Kendall felt his stomach squeeze in recognition. The man's eyes were so like his great-grandfather Armando's. "You are a runner," he declared, and grunted for Kendall to stand. "Tell me your name."

Kendall licked his lips and wished he could reach for a drink from his pouch, but he didn't dare. "Kendall," he finally replied.

The young man pursed his lips. "K'en'dl," he repeated slowly, using the clipped Keresan sounds. "That is not a name." An instant later, Kendall's right arm was twisted behind his back and the young warrior had a knife ready to slice his throat.

Kendall jerked his chin away from the glint of the knife.

"I will take you to Tubaloth," the young man whispered menacingly in his ear. "She will decide who you are and what to do with you."

Trying not to reveal his ignorance, Kendall asked, "Why Tubaloth?"

The warrior snorted. "Tubaloth is a woman who knows everything. And," he added, "Tubaloth is someone you should know."

Kendall tried not to panic. He was *not* ready for this. The miniature white mesa had lured him in like a snake waiting under a rock for a rodent. Its power had been overwhelming. He should have stayed away.

Kendall didn't dare turn his head as the young man continued to press the knife against his neck. The warrior would surely slit his throat if he did anything stupid. How could this be happening to him right in front of his own home? From what he could see, Acoma Valley looked the same. Beautiful, towering Enchanted Mesa in the distance, and Sky City on its rippling waves of rock three miles to the west of that.

"I won't fight," Kendall told him, his wrist hurting from the arm lock. "I don't plan on running. I want to go to Sky City with you."

"Sky City," he repeated. "You mean Acoma?"

Kendall swallowed and felt the cold stone weapon against his skin.

"That is a good name," the warrior conceded. "But who gave it that name?"

"I did," Kendall said. "It is my home, too."

The grip tightened and Kendall flinched.

"We shall see," was all the young man said. "But you are a runner and might try to escape."

"I promise I won't."

A female voice suddenly called from the direction of the mesa. "What are you doing, Akish?"

"Jeneum, stand back," Akish commanded. "Our enemy might be dangerous."

A scent of cedar wafted by as the girl came around the mesa and into Kendall's view. She wore a soft deerskin dress, cut loose to take advantage of cooling breezes on hot summer days. She was barefoot, her smooth legs tanned dark from the sun. Her hair was glorious, black and silky all the way to her knees. A bright blue strip of cloth held back the bulk in a thick, loose ponytail.

She was beautiful as she held her bundle of cedar branches, and Kendall realized he had forgotten to breathe. Then he felt mortified at having the girl see him with his arm locked behind his back and a knife to his throat.

Kendall wondered if she and Akish were married, although he was beginning to realize she couldn't be much older than himself.

Jeneum wrinkled her nose, studying Kendall with dark brown eyes. "Akish, he's a boy. He doesn't look very dangerous. What tribe is he, and where did you discover him?"

"Open your eyes, *tc'itc'i.*"

Sister. Akish had just called her sister.

"He wears our own apparel, and yet he is a stranger. I know every boy in the village. And so do you," he added.

She made a face at her brother. "What family do you belong to?" she asked Kendall, taking a step closer.

"Beware," Akish warned.

"Oh, put away the knife, *dyu'ma,*" she told him. "He's not going to run. Are you?"

Kendall shook his head, doing his best to keep his skin away from the blade.

"See?" Jeneum said.

Akish let out a grunting laugh. "You are too trusting." But he finally lowered the weapon, though maintaining his grip on Kendall. "Answer the question. What clan are you?"

Kendall wasn't sure what would be the correct response. The wrong one could seal his doom, but there was no choice. "I belong to the Snake Clan."

Kendall felt a slight intake of breath from his captor behind him. The knife in Akish's hand returned, and it was so close Kendall could feel the prick of pinched skin.

"I know every Snake Runner as my brother," the warrior said slowly. "How can you be Snake when I am Snake?"

A vision of his own execution flashed before Kendall's eyes.

Jeneum covered her mouth. "But, Akish," she whispered between her fingers, "he has come just in time. The snake dance begins tomorrow and *sa naicdi'a*—"

"Hush," Akish told her.

"The gods have sent him," she added, ignoring her brother.

"That is for Tubaloth to decide."

Jeneum nodded her agreement, looking into Kendall's eyes without blinking. He stared back, feeling an urge to touch the softness of her long hair. It was so much like his mother's and the way she used to wear it that he wanted to make sure Jeneum was real, that he wasn't just having the strangest dream of his life. What was the matter with him? He'd never felt this way before. He shook his head to clear his confusing thoughts. Felt the blade puncture. A drop of blood trickled down his throat.

Startled, Jeneum gave a soft cry and reached up to wipe the blood away with her finger.

"Stand back!" Akish said sternly.

She obeyed, then suddenly clutched at her brother's arm. "Look!" She pointed, directing his gaze across the desert.

Akish used a word Kendall had never heard before. Then the young man spoke, and his voice sounded awestruck. "They are back."

"Who is back?" Kendall asked, feeling blind in his poition facing the mesa and not the open desert. He sensed the sudden tension. Alarm swept over Jeneum's face, and Akish's jaw muscles flexed. Then the young warrior lowered the knife and stuck it back in the leather band on his thigh. He still grasped Kendall by the arm.

"Can we make it home before they get here?" Jeneum whispered.

"Let me see," Kendall demanded.

Akish spun him around. "There. To the northeast."

At first, Kendall couldn't see a thing, but a moment later the scene came into focus. About five miles away, figures glinted in the sunlight, raising a cloud of dust.

"They shine," Jeneum said softly.

It was true. And so odd. People traveling across the desert who actually sparkled and glimmered, their raiment catching the rays of the mid-morning sun. "How could someone shine like that?" Kendall asked.

Akish gave a brief sarcastic laugh. "They are fools to announce their presence long before they arrive."

Jeneum glanced at Kendall. "They wear suits of metal all over their bodies. From head to foot. Metal hats and metal leggings. It makes them sweat profusely. And there are no women, only men."

Some of the words she used were unfamiliar, and Kendall wasn't sure he'd understood. She described these people like they were men in space suits or something. What did Jeneum mean?

"They're coming faster," Akish said, and his grip finally dropped.

Kendall put a hand above his eyes. The shining men

were riding on horseback. That explained the cloud of dust rising from the desert.

Akish took his sister's hand and began running toward Sky City. Kendall followed, easily outrunning them in only a few moments.

After a mile, Jeneum stopped. "I can't make it. They are almost upon us."

Sure enough, the mounted horses had passed Enchanted Mesa and were closing the miles to Sky City. Now Kendall could hear and even feel the horses' pounding hooves shaking the earth. The group seemed bigger the closer it got, and he counted close to thirty horsemen.

Akish mumbled a curse.

Kendall felt exposed out in the open desert. There was nowhere to hide. They crouched near a stand of juniper, but the horsemen spotted them. A cry was raised, and the leader lifted an arm to point them out.

"There is still a mile to the lower rocks on the south side," Akish said. "From there we can climb to the top. I know a hidden trail. It's more dangerous, but we can do it."

"Oh, Akish, we can't do that!" Jeneum said. "People have been hurt climbing that trail."

"I've got an idea," Kendall said.

Akish looked at him as though he couldn't possibly have any ideas worth considering. There was also a note of surprise, as though he had expected Kendall to escape when he had the chance.

"Run to the cliffs and climb. Don't look back. I'll meet you later."

"What are you going to do?" Jeneum asked.

Her eyes on his face were unnerving, and Kendall glanced away, feeling his heart stumble inside his chest.

"Don't listen to him," Akish said, pulling his sister. "This is his chance to go. Let him."

"But, Akish!" Jeneum protested. "The strangers might hurt him."

"Don't worry, I won't be captured," Kendall told her, beginning to run again. He yelled over his shoulder. "I'm going to try to outrun them."

CHAPTER
SIX

—

"You can't do that," Jeneum cried. "You'll be trampled under their huge beasts."

Akish grabbed her hand. "He is crazy," he said, and his eyes were so cold and black that Kendall couldn't fathom what the young man was thinking.

Before he could respond, Kendall watched them race to the cliffs of Sky City, using what little scrub piñon and sagebrush dotted the sand as cover. Akish didn't look back, but Jeneum gave him one quick glance, her face torn with emotion.

"I *am* crazy," Kendall muttered as he stepped out into the open.

The riders yanked on their reins and chased after him. Kendall's long legs flew over the sand. His bare feet jumped the gently rolling ground. As the horses grew closer, his heart felt like a mallet inside his chest. He couldn't think about what would happen if they overtook him. He just ran faster, until the pain made him want to scream.

The galloping hooves became deafening. The sound of metal clashed behind his head, ringing eerily. Whipping around to look, Kendall nearly tripped and fell over.

Bearded men wearing crested metal helmets, chain mail, and steel armor chest pieces had suddenly gained on him. They began to circle.

A single horseman pulled closer, yelling foreign words.

He unsheathed a blade of silver. Fear squeezed Kendall's chest as he ducked from the flash of the sharp metal sword. Then he realized the armored man wasn't trying to hurt him with the sword, just stop him. As the man continued to shout, Kendall recognized the words he was yelling as Spanish.

Gloved hands grasped at his shoulders, but Kendall darted past the enclosing circle of armored horses. Weighed down with gear and weapons, the small army could not turn quickly enough—except for the single horseman who seemed determined to catch him. Kendall could hear the slap of the reins as the rider urged his animal forward.

They ran neck and neck, ancient magic pouring over Kendall. He was back with the runners of his ancestors at last, and the power consumed him, gave him strength and speed like nothing else ever had before. Kendall could have sworn he was flying across the ground. He'd never run this fast. But he hadn't had to outrun a horse before. Even a horse slowed down by bedrolls and armor.

Frustration crossed the Spanish soldier's face, and he gave another mighty smack against his horse's back. Thick, dried white streaks covered the animal's flanks as he tried to obey, nostrils spread wide, snorting. Wet lather coated the horse now, running down his legs.

The Spaniard shouted through his matted red beard. ¡Alto! ¡Alto, savajo!"

Kendall ignored him. He wasn't planning on getting captured just when he'd arrived. These were the days his great-grandfather hadn't been able to tell him about before he died. The days when the Snake Clan was alive and strong. Before it began to shrink toward extinction.

Cutting over to the lower cliff rock, Kendall scurried up

the sloping path to the toe- and footholds that would take
him to the top. Halfway up the sheer side of the mesa, he
slowed down. His heart slammed against his rib cage, and it
was hard to control his shaking leg muscles as fatigue hit.

He heard shouts below as the horsemen regrouped and
dismounted. It would take time to tie up their horses, un-
load their armor, and begin a slow, unfamiliar ascent of the
steep cliffs of Acoma.

Kendall gulped in air as he clung to the side of the mesa,
waiting for his legs to calm their fierce trembling. The steps
chiseled into the rock helped keep him from falling. He got
going again, and the path twisted near the top. Kendall
climbed around a boulder, then stumbled up the last few
steps, reaching the summit and the village.

The aroma of fresh bread filled the air, lingering from the
morning's baking. Heat shimmered against the mud walls of
the two- and three-story attached houses. Homemade ladders constructed of piñon branches leaned against the outside walls of the first story of each house, as familiar as they
were in the future. But front doors did not exist here in the
past. Instead, there was a circular hole in the center of each
roof with the rungs of another ladder sticking out of the
opening. In times of trouble, the ladders could be pulled
down and the opening closed off for safety from invaders.

Even so, Kendall could almost swear there had been no
time change. Perhaps it had only been the heat playing
with his mind, only the gut-wrenching magic swirling so
powerfully at the miniature enchanted mesa. But deep down
he knew differently. He was in his own time no longer. The
mesa had thrown him backward several hundred years. There
was no doubt the gods ruled this valley.

At the edge of the village, Kendall collapsed onto the sun-baked ground. A hot breeze lifted the sweaty hair off his neck. He felt dizzy from running so frantically. Down below, the Spanish conquistadors shouted. A cloudless blue sky dazzled above, even as the distant sounds of sixteenth-century armor and neighing cavalry drifted upward. It seemed unreal.

He pictured Dad going into his bedroom to wake him up and finding his bed empty. What would his father think? What would he do? Was the present continuing at the same time the past replayed itself? Or perhaps the future stood still while he was here? That seemed to make more sense. When he returned through the enchanted passageway of the mesa, he would return to the same night—yesterday—when Brett had dropped him off. At least he hoped so.

Akish and Jeneum appeared in front of him.

"Come with me, Snake boy," the young man commanded, wrenching Kendall to his feet.

Standing behind her brother, Jeneum smiled at Kendall. "I have never seen a runner like you before."

Akish pulled Kendall through the narrow streets, his grip like iron. "He is a magician, my sister. Don't believe what you see."

"He is a great and mighty Snake Runner," Jeneum said, glancing at Kendall.

"A sorcerer knows how to charm the desert and his feet. And now you," her brother added.

"But he ran like the wind," Jeneum said. "He flew over the earth like a bird and raced those powerful beasts."

"I have never seen such a feat before either," Akish finally admitted. Kendall wished he could figure out what Akish's problem was. The young man had been defending his home when he first saw Kendall, but now he heard reluctant awe in his voice. Maybe jealousy, too.

"I didn't know I could do that," Kendall said under his breath.

Akish stopped on the street. "What did you say?"

Kendall held still, realizing he'd spoken in English.

"Do you see?" Akish barked at Jeneum. "He comes from another tribe. He's an imposter. I have never heard that language. Not from any of the Big River tribes to the east, nor from the Head Pounders who raid us."

Kendall wanted to kick himself for messing up like that. What a stupid thing to do. More than stupid, it was perilous. He could get killed for mistakes like that.

"I have been lost and learned another language while I was gone," Kendall said in an effort to explain, feeling ignorant as he stumbled over the Acoma words.

Akish didn't look convinced, but Jeneum paused as they came to the village square, empty under the hot sun. "Brother, this Snake Runner is not all bad. He saved us, too."

Akish looked away, and Kendall knew the young man was not willing to admit anything more at the moment.

"There's no time to talk now," Akish said. "We must hurry to the Antelope House before the shining metal men reach the top of the rock. We must warn everyone."

Kendall turned down the row of houses toward the clan house of the Antelope. The Antelope Clan was the head clan, the leaders of the Acoma people. The chief of the tribe lived there. Akish grabbed Kendall's arm, swinging him around to face him.

"What are you doing?" Akish demanded.

"Going to the clan house of the Antelope."

"How do you know this is the direction?"

Kendall paused, wondering if he was going the right way or the wrong way. He had instinctively turned to where the house was in the Sky City he knew, but whether it was in the same place now was a good question.

"Because I know—I told you I'm Acoma," he finished.

Akish's jaw set. "You are right. This is the way."

Jeneum glanced downward, suppressing a smile.

"But," Akish said, glaring into Kendall's face, "you will follow me. Understand?"

Kendall nodded. "Sure. Right."

Akish began to run. Kendall could feel his urgency. Once they reached the Antelope Clan house, Akish climbed the ladder leaning against the outside wall. He reached the roof of the first story in seconds and called out to see if anyone was home. From the bottom of the interior ladder, an old woman's voice echoed upward, giving Akish permission to enter.

Kendall stood silently with Jeneum on the street. He couldn't help glancing at her from the corner of his eye. Kendall didn't think he'd ever seen such a pretty girl.

When Akish climbed back down the ladder, he brought bad news. "I knew that everyone was in the fields, but I panicked. I thought the Antelope chief would take charge of this, but he is not back yet. A runner has already left to warn them."

A young woman carrying a painted clay jug on her head stepped up from the rocks below the cliff line, returning from the water cisterns.

Jeneum spoke behind Kendall. "Pekah must have spotted the strangers."

The girl named Pekah paused when she reached them.

"The shining strangers are back. Hurry home," she advised. She quickly walked down the street of homes, then climbed up one of the outside ladders leaning against the mud-brick wall. Kendall could see the top of her head as she reached the roof; then she disappeared down the inner ladder.

The streets were fast becoming deserted. Playing children were pulled away by their mothers. Even the elderly sitting in the shade suddenly climbed their ladders and vanished inside their homes. The summer afternoon grew hotter and more still as the village streets emptied.

Suddenly, the sounds of armor and metal rang from the direction of the rock trail.

"Go, Jeneum," Akish said.

His sister obeyed, hurrying down the row of houses and then turning a corner. Kendall wondered if he would ever see her again. He wanted to say something, even just goodbye, but she was gone.

"What do the strangers want?" Kendall asked Akish.

"What do you think? They want our years of stored food, our gifts from the gods."

"How many times have they come before?"

"Twice. The first was only a season ago, but many stories come from the Big River tribes. Groups of them stop to ask for food and blankets and corn. Some stay for days and weeks at a time, but the villages near the river have no choice when they camp right next to them."

"Are you afraid?" The eerie clanging sound of the Spaniards' metal and their polished swords frightened Kendall, and he couldn't help asking.

Akish gave Kendall a strange look. "I am not afraid of

hem. Why should I be? We live on the safest spot for hundreds of miles. There are more than a thousand of us and only a small group of them. And"—Akish paused to eye Kendall—"we have the blessings of the gods. The metal men do not have any of these things. They will soon tire of their travels and go back where they came from. We give them such little food it will not be worth it to come here again."

Kendall shook his head. "No, they will not go back. They have come too far. They will want the land and precious stones and metals that are here. They will stay."

Akish suddenly laughed. "I think you are unwise, K'en'dl. The strangers cannot even tolerate Father Sun. They wear too many clothes with their metal suits, sweating just like their beasts."

Akish held Kendall back against the wall of the plaza and squatted down on the rocky ground. "Be quiet, and don't say a word."

A dozen Spaniards clattered into the open square. Their stale, sweaty smell carried across the air. They looked weary in the heavy armor. Still wearing their helmets, they now also carried swords and heavy revolvers with long barrels.

Then Kendall saw a native man wearing a breechcloth talking with the group of soldiers.

Akish muttered, "That is their interpreter. He is from one of the Big River tribes. They call him Tomas. I call him a traitor to learn so many languages and make friends with all the tribes. Someday it will lead to war."

"It seems like it would be a good thing to know what the strangers say," Kendall said. "And find out what they want."

"I do not wish to speak with them. If they can't communicate with us, they will get frustrated and go away."

This was naive on Akish's part, Kendall thought. Wishful thinking.

The group of Spaniards worked their way down the rows of homes. The warriors who stood sentry at each of Acoma's trails followed them. At each home, the interpreter climbed the outside ladder until he reached the roof, then called "*Guatzi!*" down the shadowy circular opening, using the familiar greeting.

House to house the group of Spaniards went, watched carefully by the Acoma sentries. Baskets of corn and ground flour were lifted through the roof openings. Sometimes a turkey or dried jerky, animal skins or blankets. Fast, frenzied Spanish flowed through the group as they distributed the food among themselves and continued down the narrow village streets.

It was eerie watching the Spaniards move through the village, and Kendall knew he was watching history play out before his eyes.

"They have traveled for many months from the lands south and have run out of supplies," Akish said. "We have heard stories of their caravans and animals, but they are stupid not to bring enough."

"They should start farming like we do," Kendall said, thinking out loud. Now *he* was being wishful. The Spaniards wouldn't settle with families and farms for another hundred years. These men were here only to take riches back to Spain and claim the land—land that belonged to people who already lived here.

Akish's face set into hard lines. "They aren't farmers.

hey are warriors, part of an army who come in place of an nvisible ruler."

A moment later, Akish jumped up from his watchful po- ition and ran down a side street. Kendall hurried after him.

Akish scrambled up a sturdy ladder near the end of a row f houses and paused at the roof opening. He spoke the tra- litional words used to request entry, identifying himself to hose below. "May I come in, *tc'itc'i?*"

Jeneum's voice spoke through the opening. "Come in, ny brother. And bring the runner with you."

The young man ignored Kendall as he descended the adder, but Kendall followed him anyway, carefully stepping lown the rungs out of the bright sunshine into shadows. After his eyes adjusted to the dim interior, he saw Jeneum tanding near the fire in her white deerskin dress.

The main room was about ten feet by twelve feet with mmaculately swept rock floors. Whitewashed brick walls nelped lighten the room. Baskets of food, piles of tanned eather, and two rabbits waiting to be skinned lined the valls. In one corner the long rectangular grinding stones nad been washed and put away for the day. Kendall caught glimpses of massive food preparation for the pending cere- nonies of the next few days. His stomach growled, and he realized he was starving. When was the last time he'd eaten?

Burger King last night with Brett. About eighteen hours ago. Eighteen hours—a lifetime.

"Where's *Nai'ya?*" Akish asked.

"Our mother is grinding corn at Hora's home," his sister replied.

"I hope they are safe."

"The metal warriors are not hurting anyone," Jeneum

said. "They have never done anything wrong. Their hair faces and metal clothes are frightening, but we can't refus food to people who are hungry."

"They should not be here. Something bad will happen. Akish predicted.

Kendall stepped forward. "Stop. You're scaring her."

"Stay out of this, runner *tca taka*," Akish said, callin Kendall "boy."

Kendall felt his face burn. He turned away, shakin his head.

Jeneum glanced upward when heavy footsteps sounde across the roof above them. "What should we do?" sh asked in a low voice.

Akish picked up his bow. "I will run them out of here. refuse to give them any more. Our storage rooms are bein depleted."

A loud male voice called through the opening.

Akish remained silent, his bow and arrow shaking in hi hands. Jeneum's eyes pleaded with her brother. Kendal could feel her helplessness. Finally, Akish threw down hi weapon, yielding to his sister. She went to the corner, wher another ladder led downstairs to the cooler storage rooms.

Akish paced the floor until she returned with a filled bas ket of yellow-and-blue ears of winter corn. Jeneum set it a the foot of the steps, then ran across the room and disap peared up the ladder to a second floor.

"Take it up to them," Akish ordered Kendall, pointing t the corn. "And get the basket back. We have already give away three."

Kendall was startled at the request. His Keresan was poo

and he didn't want to face the Spanish conquistadors, but Akish wasn't budging. He just stared at him, almost like it was a dare.

Finally he picked up the basket and ascended the ladder rungs, breaking into hot sunshine again. Hands grabbed the basket out of his arms, and he jumped onto the roof, almost falling backward.

Tomas, the interpreter, turned to the Spaniards' leader and spoke. The leader had a reddish brown beard on his sweat-streaked face. Wearing full armor, mud-caked black boots, and a sword at his waist, he stepped forward, speaking rapidly.

The interpreter asked, "Is this all you have to give? Yours is the last house."

Kendall nodded.

The Spanish leader sighed heavily and handed the corn down to another man.

Kendall reached for the basket, but Tomas said, "They need it to carry the food on their horses. Tell the household they are grateful."

Right, Kendall thought.

Another soldier swung around and pointed at Kendall, a flood of Spanish pouring from his lips.

Kendall stepped back, suddenly recognizing him. It was the man on the horse whom he'd raced across the desert. He started for the ladder, ducking his head down, but Tomas stopped him, looking uncomfortable, and interpreted the Spanish words.

"He says you must be part animal to run like a beast in the desert."

Kendall stared at him. "I make a better horse than his own does."

The Spaniard waited for Tomas to translate the words. Kendall knew he should have kept his mouth shut. He took another step toward the ladder, hoping to escape any further dangerous conversation.

Laughter broke out among the soldiers when they heard the interpretation.

There was shame on Tomas's face as he translated the new Spanish to Kendall. "He says if you're that good, perhaps he should take you with them and turn you into his own personal donkey."

A second man jostled forward, speaking rapid Spanish and lifting a gauntleted hand.

Tomas added, "They say you are taller than most of the others, and your eyes are different."

Man, this wasn't good. Kendall felt his chest heave.

Another jesting comment was yelled from the crowd of soldiers on the street. Kendall saw Tomas wince.

"What do they say now?" he asked, knowing he should just ignore it.

Tomas wouldn't look him in the eye as he spoke the Keresan interpretation. "They want to touch your hair and skin and see if you are a real man or a beast."

Kendall put a hand on the ladder. "Why do you do this for them?"

Tomas turned his face away before he answered. "They pay me well."

"Tell them I am enchanted," Kendall said. "A horse in disguise."

Tomas's mouth twitched in a smile. He repeated the words, and the soldiers laughed at Kendall's joke. Finally, the leader with the red beard barked a command to his men.

In low tones, Tomas said, "They are leaving now."

Kendall tasted relief in his mouth.

Placing a foot on the ladder's top rung, Kendall waited only long enough to see the group of Spaniards jostle their way down the village road as they returned to the trail. They would probably spill the food trying to get down the cliff walls. It meant only that they would be back for more that much sooner.

Kendall had barely made it down the ladder before Ikish pushed him back up.

"It is time to see Tubaloth. She will decree what we should do with you."

CHAPTER
SEVEN

Afternoon sun slanted across the streets as the residents of
Acoma arrived back from the fields. Carrying sticks and
hoes, the men and women climbed the rock trails and dispersed to their homes for the evening meal.

Furtive whisperings flew among neighbors when news of
the Spaniards' sudden visit spread throughout the village.
Extra sentries were ordered at each trail around the perimeter of the village.

The elders of the tribe gathered in the head kiva of the
Antelope Clan. Kendall watched Akish descend the ladder
and enter, leaving him to wait at the roof's opening with another man acting as his guard. Kendall crouched in the twilight, knowing he wasn't going to run. What if the warriors
thought he was a Spanish spy? His appearance on the same
day as theirs might make people suspicious.

Smells of roasting corn and frying meat came from the
rooftops as wives and daughters prepared the evening meal.
Kendall felt uneasy, wondering about his fate. He got up to
pace the rooftop, but the guard stepped in front of him.
Kendall sat down again to show him he wasn't intending to
run or fight.

His head whirred with a thousand thoughts. He had come
here accidentally, without a plan. He needed to convince
them that he wasn't a spy and didn't mean any harm. But

hat if they didn't believe his story? They might be planning his execution right now. Should he try to make a break for it and get back home? The possibilities and ideas were endless as they shot through his mind.

He could still feel the powerful pull of the mesa. What a shock it had been to find that his prayer stick had disappeared, left in the future when the enchanted passageway carried him to the past. Kendall had the feeling that his traveling back in time wasn't an accident. Perhaps the gods had planned his destiny. He was here at a time when the Snake Clan was strong, and he suddenly had the chance to learn about the ancient ways.

Kendall wished he could hear what they were saying inside the kiva. He knew the future of Acoma wasn't good. Akish hoped the conquistador soldiers would eventually go away, but they were not going away, ever. Kendall could try to tell the villagers again, but they might not believe him.

He was a stranger, even in his leather skins and carrying the Snake Runner's sacred bundle. He was sure his Anglo features showed in small ways—his lighter skin, his taller height. It was probably one of the things that made Akish so suspicious.

The ladder creaked as the young man reappeared. "You are to be taken to Tubaloth's home. It will be her decision whether you stay with the Acoma people as a friend or whether you will be kept as a slave."

Kendall nodded. He could be a slave if he had to.

Akish leaned closer, not finished. "Or if you shall be left to die in the desert."

Kendall grunted at the Snake warrior, trying not to let

his fear show. If they took him back to the desert for th
roving wolves or cougars, he would just run to the mesa ar
return home. But the nagging thought he'd been pushir
away all day broke through: What if he couldn't *get* bac
home? Would the power work in the opposite direction–
from the past back to the future?

He couldn't think about that right now. It had to wor
again, but not yet. Right now he didn't want to go bac
The thought of Juanita, so proud of her Spanish ancestor
living with his father in his mother's room, sleeping in he
bed, using her possessions, drove him crazy with fury ar
jealousy. He wanted to see his dad and fix things betwee
them, but that would have to wait. Kendall wasn't ready t
face him. Besides, Dad was the one that had turned away.

Kendall sighed, feeling the peace he always felt here
Acoma was his home. This was where he belonged, an
these were his people. He closed his eyes, bringing back th
vision of his mother and the last time he'd seen his grea
grandfather as a young Acoma runner. He knew they wer
here with him. Somehow everything would be all right. I
he wasn't killed first.

Akish added, "Lehonti and Ogath are going with us t
see Tubaloth."

Two men climbed up through the kiva roof, then dow
the outside ladder. Kendall recognized one of them as
medicine man carrying his buckskin bag of herbal med
cine, eagle feathers, and small bowls. They didn't speal
only led Akish and Kendall through the darkening stree
and across the open square.

The elders stopped at a home in the middle of a long ro

of three-story houses. They climbed the outside ladder, and Kendall followed behind them to the roof. Lehonti suddenly turned, his black eyes glittering under starlight.

"There is no one else like Tubaloth. As a young girl, she was struck by lightning—and lived. That is the sign from the gods of her calling. She is one of the great ones. Be careful, and be wise."

Kendall nodded to him, swallowing the fear lodged in his throat. The solemn words only increased his apprehension. He wanted to slow things down. He needed time to think about everything that had happened to him. He had to figure out what to say, but there was no time. He was being swept away, taken over by the strange events and people of this day. The power of the magic had taken over his life. Suddenly, there were bearded conquistadors, ancient medicine men, suspicious Snake clansmen. His life was out of his control. Ever since Akish had pressed an arrow against his throat.

Ogath called down to the household inhabitants.

A female voice greeted them and asked them to enter. A small fire burned in the pit at the south wall, throwing shadows against the smooth white walls. The bright, square room was neat and orderly. Dinner had already been eaten, and a young woman was cleaning up. She gestured for the four of them to sit while she finished.

Kendall was surprised when she climbed up the inner ladder to the second floor and didn't return. Long minutes passed. Akish and the other elders didn't speak. Kendall's stomach growled, and Akish glared at him. The other two men acted as if they hadn't heard.

Finally, the woman reappeared, but she never looked at them as she went up the center ladder that led to the outside roof. Kendall couldn't understand what was going on. Why had Tubaloth left them sitting alone in her house? A moment later, he heard the creak of the inner ladder as another person descended from the upper rooms.

Outlined by the light of the fire's flames, a tiny, ancient woman entered the room. Long white hair thin as lace fell to her knees. A beautifully embroidered deerskin robe brushed the floor. Her face was a mass of fine wrinkles crisscrossed over her cheeks and throat. Blue-veined fingers reached out to acknowledge the group of men sitting cross-legged on the floor, but she didn't speak a word.

Kendall felt his stomach drop. The old woman scared him. He wanted to glance at Akish, hoping the young man would tell him what to do, but Kendall didn't dare move his head. Akish wouldn't help him anyway. This was his test. What he said or did would determine his fate.

Tubaloth settled on a wooden bench by the fire and nodded to Ogath.

The medicine man rose and prepared a space near the fire, opening the bags tied to his waist. After cleaning a spot on the floor, he drew a sand painting, chanting a drawing song as he worked on the details of sky and turtles and raindrops. The sand painting was a gesture of greeting and respect to Tubaloth, a blessing of rain, good fortune, and health to the household. When he finished, the elderly woman inspected his work, then beckoned Kendall to kneel in front of her. He obeyed, his turquoise necklace bouncing against his bare chest.

68

Tubaloth reached out and fingered the deep blue stone, then lifted his sacred bundle to weigh it gently in her hands. She didn't open it, just nodded her head, her breath raspy as she examined it with elegant age-spotted hands.

She set down the bundle, then spoke at last. Her voice was strong. "Tell me why you wear this blue precious stone."

Kendall glanced around nervously, but her eyes compelled his gaze back to her face. "My great-grandfather gave it to me."

"What was his name?"

"I—I . . ." Kendall paused, thoughts speeding through his mind. How could he explain that future Spaniards would take away their Acoma names and give them all new Spanish names? Finally, he answered, "His name was Armando."

Tubaloth never blinked. "I don't recall hearing that name before."

Kendall didn't respond, figuring it was best to stay quiet unless she asked him a specific question.

The old woman seemed to read this thoughts. It was disconcerting. "And the stone?"

"It is the color of the heavens, symbolic of Father Sky," Kendall told her.

The medicine woman nodded. "Tell me what your most sacred item is in the bundle at your waist."

"My great-grandfather gave me an ear of pure white corn, blessed by our mother, *Iatuk*."

"Your grandfather taught you well. May I meet him? Where does he live?"

Kendall shook his head. "He used to live here at Acoma. I mean—" Now he'd done it. He couldn't tell her that

Armando would live hundreds of years from now, that he hadn't even been born yet. Kendall bowed his head. "He lives no more."

Tubaloth leaned forward and breathed in Kendall's face, her white hair falling over one shoulder to sweep the floor. "He is with the gods and has helped bring a vision to me."

At the medicine woman's words, Akish and the other men shifted in their seats.

"He was Snake, and so are you, boy-man."

"Yes," Kendall whispered.

"The Snake Clan sits closest to the gods who bring us life. Theirs is a sacred task of life-giving rain." Tubaloth leaned forward, raised a finger, and placed it directly on Kendall's forehead. Her face came closer. Kendall tried to gaze back without blinking but couldn't, glancing down instead at the old woman's bare feet laced with blue and black veins.

She raised his chin with her hand, forcing him to look at her. "Last night there was disruption in Acoma Valley. I could feel it coming through K'atzim'o, Enchanted Mesa, and its twin child-mesa to the south."

Kendall sucked in his breath. She knew the spot where time had let him through.

Tubaloth leaned back, knowledge that she had struck a chord showing clearly on her face. "I had a dream, a vision of a messenger."

At her words Akish's leather clothing rustled. Kendall was sure the young warrior would like to see him fed to the wolves piece by piece.

"Change is coming to this village," Tubaloth prophesied.

"First there will be famine. But the strangers will demand more than our meager stores of food. They will want our hearts, our loyalties, and then our home on our beautiful rock."

The elders grunted in agreement, but the aged medicine woman didn't pause to acknowledge them.

"I know the gods are watching over us because I was told in my dream that a messenger would come. Someone who would give us hope that Acoma would always be here, even after the evil that the strangers bring."

Kendall could see Akish squirming.

"With great respect, Tubaloth," Akish said, "who is this messenger who will save us?"

"This messenger is not a savior," she informed him. "Only a messenger of hope for future generations. I saw the person in my vision. Saw his countenance and sacred stone of the blue sky."

Her hands fell from Kendall's face. She looked at each man sitting in her home. "This boy-man who kneels at my feet is the messenger," she declared.

CHAPTER
EIGHT

Jeneum had bowls of rabbit stew, hunks of bread, and roasted corn waiting for Akish and Kendall when they arrived home. Embers smoldered in the stone hearth, giving a golden glow.

In one corner, Akish's mother, Sharid, mended clothing. She acknowledged Kendall with a nod and soft smile when he came down the ladder but didn't speak. She was small and squarely built with black hair tied tightly against the back of her head.

Kendall sat cross-legged on the floor next to Akish and dug into the food. Ravenous, he ate and ate until his stomach felt like it would burst. Jeneum kept serving, but finally Akish put up a hand to stop her.

"Thank you, *tc'itc'i*," Akish said. "You are a fine cook, and will make your future husband very happy."

Jeneum smiled and blushed, picking up the pottery bowls and sweeping the area clean of crumbs.

During Jeneum's cleaning, their mother disappeared upstairs to retire, and Kendall couldn't stop himself from asking Akish where their father was.

Sitting close to the fire, Akish sharpened his knife. "He died on a hunting expedition when Jeneum was still a child."

"I'm sorry," Kendall said, hoping he hadn't caused pain by bringing it up.

"It is my responsibility to farm and hunt for my family,"

Akish said. "And I need to help Jeneum find a good husband. There are many young men who are watching her, and it will not be long until there are proposals for marriage at our doorstep."

"I have heard of that, gifts laid at a doorstep from a young man to the woman he loves."

Akish nodded, laying down his knife. "Last week one of my Snake brothers left jewelry and blankets and an entire deer for Pekah, Jeneum's friend. I think it will be Jeneum's turn soon."

Kendall knew Jeneum listened as her brother talked about her future, but she was silent as she stirred the last of the fire and took down the sleeping rolls hanging from the walls. Her silky black hair swirled across her back as she went about her tasks. It reminded Kendall of his mother's silhouette. Sometimes it felt so long ago, and yet there were moments, especially now, when Kendall could remember so clearly. His mother felt very near.

"My father was a Snake Priest," Akish told Kendall. "For the first time I will be taking his place during the ceremonies tomorrow. You will be a runner at my side, messenger boy-man."

Kendall's head snapped up at the words. He was sure Akish wanted to question him about who he was and where he came from, but Tubaloth's words seemed to have taken away his hostility.

Then Kendall saw that Akish had noticed Kendall looking at Jeneum as she worked around the house. It was hard not to gaze at her, but Kendall realized he had to be careful. There were probably other young men in the village who wouldn't welcome him if they already had affections for the beautiful girl.

"I will find a brave warrior for my sister, a good hunter, one who has a fine home." Akish's words seemed to challenge any intentions Kendall might have.

Kendall followed Akish up the opening to the rooftop. Jeneum spread their blankets into beds, her small figure a shadow in the darkness. Stars glittered in a black, moonless sky.

"Sleep well," Jeneum said, then climbed over to the second roof and joined her mother.

"She seems so young to be thinking of marriage."

"No more talking." Akish rolled over and went to sleep.

Kendall lay on his back watching the night sky. Tubaloth's words crowded his mind. How could he be a messenger when he didn't even know what the message was? As a skilled runner, he was invited to participate in the snake ceremony, but he didn't even know what he would need to do. That sacred knowledge had died with his great-grandfather.

What had caused the Snake Clan to die out? Akish had indicated it was a strong clan with many runners and Snake Priests. But in the future his clan became extinct, and nobody here knew that he was the last living member. Since children were born into the clan of their mother, Kendall would need to marry a Snake Clan girl. There *were* no Snake Clan girls in the future.

Restless, Kendall rose from his blanket and walked to the edge of the roof. Across the valley, *K'atzim'o* glowed white and spectacular. He heard Tubaloth's words again in his mind. *I was told in my dream that a messenger would come.*

Kendall pulled off his turquoise necklace and held it up, searching the sky. "Grandfather, Mother. What does it mean? I have no message."

The skies were silent, the night deep and strangely still. Kendall crouched on the ground and quietly whispered the words he'd been thinking all evening. "I want to stay. Tell the gods to let me stay."

It was still dark when Akish woke Kendall. He'd gone to sleep with images of snakes and the ceremonies filling his dreams. Kendall felt eager, yet nervous. He and Akish rolled up their beds and returned downstairs to hang them on a large pole in the corner of the room.

After washing, Akish laid two large bundles wrapped in leather on the main floor and untied the cords that held them closed. He unfolded the first layer. "Today I will wear my father's clothing, and you will wear mine."

Memories from a year ago on the roof with his great-grandfather washed over him. Kendall knew that he and Akish were going to perform the preparation rites for running just as Armando had done for him the very first time. The emotions were so strong and the memories so sweet that he had a hard time keeping back the tears that burned his eyes.

Kendall removed his own leather girdle and put on the leather apron Akish handed him. The soft deerskin had been painted with yellow and black lines across the top and bottom. Between these lines a black snake outlined in white wriggled across the front.

"I made the apron with my father," Akish told him. "The stripes are the rainbow that follows a storm. The prints inside the snake represent the frog that returns with the rain. Next, we put on the *i'picty a*."

Kendall watched Akish mix a bowl of white powder with water. Using his fingers, Akish painted lightning bolts on Kendall's upper arms, then painted his mouth and chin white. "Your mouth must be made pure for the snakes."

Kendall jerked his head up. Pure mouths for the snakes? What did that mean? Kendall didn't dare ask, but his palms began to sweat as he wondered what would happen out in the desert. And what about the snake dance afterward? These next few days were going to be vital to the rest of his life. His great-grandfather had never been able to do the snake ceremonies because there had been no other Snake clansman alive during his lifetime. Kendall had been given a blessing from the gods. He had to remember that, even if he was terrified.

"Now you paint me," Akish commanded.

Kendall dipped his fingers into the bowl and copied the lightning bolts onto Akish's arms.

"We will make our arms and hands white up to the elbow. Then they will be pure to hold the snakes."

There was just enough *i'picty a* for both of them to finish.

Akish bent down and picked up two fat necklaces of beads and stones, six strands tied together. Kendall took one of them and put it around his own neck next to the turquoise necklace. Then Akish showed him how to tie the embroidered sash around his waist on the right side to secure his sacred bundle. Just above the right knee, he strapped a tortoise-shell rattle. Bracelets and anklets of beads and sea-shells went on Kendall's wrists and ankles.

Unfolding the last part of the bundle, Akish lifted two headdresses of precious golden-eagle feathers.

Kendall was in awe at the majestic splendor, soft feathers, and intricate design. "They're wonderful."

Akish fastened one to the crown of Kendall's head, leaving his hair hanging down his back except for one loop that helped secure the headdress. "My father and I made them the last winter he was alive."

At last Akish picked up the final items, soft buckskin whips about three feet long with frayed pieces of leather on the ends. Akish didn't say what they were for, and Kendall didn't ask. He couldn't think ahead to what he would be required to do with the snakes. He had to focus on this one step at a time and pray the gods would help him when it was time.

"Now we will make *ha tcamun'i*," Akish said.

Prayer sticks. Kendall had learned how to carve these with his great-grandfather, but today he took extra care.

Akish's *ha tcamun'i* was exquisitely carved in the shape of a slithering snake. The young man began to paint the diamond markings of a rattlesnake on the wood stick, including the reptile's black eyes.

Kendall sharpened the knife Akish lent him and cut his prayer stick into the same snake shape. After an hour of shaping and cutting, Kendall tied feathers to the ends and tucked the stick into his waistband.

When they finished, Jeneum and her mother served them a breakfast of corn mush and gave them bread to take with them.

Kendall followed Akish down the ladder to the head

kiva of the Snake Clan. The rising sun shot over the ring of mesas to the east, washing the world in brilliant orange light.

In keeping with custom, a line of cornmeal had been drawn around the ceremonial chamber. No one except initiated Snake Clan was allowed to cross it. Akish stepped over the line without hesitation, then turned to look at Kendall.

Kendall paused, wondering if Akish would believe he was really an initiated man. Was it only a few weeks ago when the floor had opened up to swallow him? Here he was about to enter this same kiva again.

At that moment, Tubaloth walked by, carrying her clay water jar down to the cisterns. Her white hair hung down her back in a single long braid. She paused to watch Kendall, not speaking, hooded eyes peeking out from under the shawl she wore over her head.

"Go, boy-man," she told him, then resumed her steps to the cliff trail.

Kendall stepped over the cornmeal to enter the kiva. Tubaloth seemed to know everything about him.

About three dozen Snake Priests and Snake Runners had met in the kiva chamber. The other men looked at Kendall, and a few greeted him with nods. Because of Tubaloth's decree, it seemed as though he was accepted. But he knew he would be watched to see just how well he performed and for what purpose he had come to Acoma.

Songs and prayers marked the beginning of the four days of running.

One of the older men spoke. "We must gather the finest snakes. Cleanse your thoughts and bodies and pray in purity so that our brother-serpents will send our messages to the rain gods."

Kendall wondered what they were going to do. Find snakes out in the desert and pray over them? And what kind of snakes? Tame ones, he hoped, like garter or gopher snakes. But Akish's prayer stick was decorated like a rattler.

The Snake Priest gave Kendall a leather sack, a small whip, and a bundle of eagle feathers tied together. "The feathers will soften the anger of the snake," Akish told him.

Kendall stared at him. Akish sounded serious. Kendall didn't intend to get close to any angry snakes, and he pushed away the feeling of panic rising in his gut.

As the Snake Runners filed out of the kiva, the women and children of the village climbed up to the rooftops to watch them depart for the desert.

Kendall jogged with the others, following Akish through the narrow village roads toward the cliff path. He caught sight of Jeneum as they passed. She lifted her hand in farewell. Kendall resisted the urge to acknowledge her. None of the other runners paid any attention to the watching villagers.

After scrambling down the cliff steps and toeholds, Kendall watched the group of runners head to the north. The long shadows of night disappeared behind the huge boulders standing like sentinels on the desert floor. Kendall would follow in a few minutes, but first he had something he needed to do.

Breaking away from the pack of running Snake men, he sprinted across the desert toward K'atzim'o, Enchanted Mesa. Akish followed him, and even though Kendall knew it wasn't a race, he wanted to reach the sacred spire first.

He heard the young man cry out behind him, and the anger was unmistakable. Right now Kendall didn't care, and he didn't stop until he reached the rocky shale bottom of the mesa. His heart pulsed in his throat as he took a sip from his leather water pouch.

A moment later, Akish grabbed him by the shoulder and swung him around, swiftly pulling out his knife. "I've been waiting for your first mistake, boy-man. You have gone east instead of north, you fool. You will ruin the entire ceremony! Now you will come with me. I plan to return and expose you to Tubaloth and the elders as a traitor and imposter."

CHAPTER

NINE

Kendall jerked his arm from Akish's grip. "Put the knife away. I am no fool. I ran east purposely. *K'atzim'o* is my sacred mesa, and I am going to place my prayer stick here."

Akish's jaw flexed and he threw up his hands, but he didn't question Kendall's spiritual motives. The young Acoma warrior stood without speaking as Kendall climbed the side of Enchanted Mesa. It didn't take long to find an empty recess to hold his *ha tcamun'i*. Kendall pushed the carved snake inside, remembering the first time he'd done this as his great-grandfather watched from the rocks below. He paused, holding tight to the sheer cliff wall, and bowed his head in silent prayer. His throat tightened as he heard his great-grandfather's voice in his memory. If only Armando could be with him now in the past days of the Snake Clan. They could run together.

When he reached the base again, Akish was staring at him. "You knew just where to put it."

Kendall barely looked at him. He watched the clouds brush the sky above the sheer walls of the mesa, feeling the hot sun and listening for the spirits of those he could not see.

"Perhaps you really are Acoma," Akish said, and there was a hint of respect in his voice.

"I have run to *K'atzim'o* many times. It has spoken to me before. But it was—another time."

"Perhaps you will tell me about it someday."

Kendall nodded. "Perhaps."

"I will put my own prayers here also."

Kendall waited until Akish finished placing his own prayer stick, then they ran again, retracing their steps past the cliffs of Acoma and following the other runners to the north.

They ran side by side for several miles, not speaking, matching their strides, breathing hard and even. After an hour, they stopped to drink from their water pouches.

"This is a good place to look for snakes," Akish said, tying his leather bag around his waist.

Kendall nodded, unfastening his own snake sack to hide his apprehension.

Akish knew just where to find the signs of snake tracks and follow them to the snake's home. He knew which holes had been deserted and which snakes were waiting for the Snake Runners. He knew how to sit still and wait and watch, patient as a rock on the desert floor.

Most of the time they didn't speak, not wanting to startle the snakes that would eventually crawl from their holes. But it was a good silence. It seemed they had finally made some peace.

"Ah, he comes," Akish whispered at last, sitting up on his haunches.

Kendall didn't move, didn't even breathe. A bull snake slithered from the hole they'd been watching, the back of his head opposite where they were sitting. The snake paused as though sensing the air for unusual smells and vibrations. The reptile wriggled farther out of his home, body curling like a sash.

Akish darted forward and grabbed the snake behind the head, holding its mouth open and wrapping the four-foot tail around his arm.

"Hey!" Kendall couldn't help shouting in admiration.

Akish smiled back. "Now we will find your snake over in those rocks."

By the time they had settled again on the boulders to wait, Akish had tamed the bull snake, calming him with his voice and touch. As Kendall watched the young warrior, he felt just as mesmerized as the snake.

"This is how my father did it," Akish said, stroking his bull snake like a pet.

"I hope I will be able to do as well as you."

"You will, Snake boy."

The afternoon grew warmer and Kendall wiped the sweat trickling down his forehead. Dark clouds hovered in the sky all day but eventually moved north without releasing a single drop of moisture.

They ate their meal of bread and dried venison and climbed higher into the rocks. Suddenly, Akish raised a hand to point out a snake warming itself on the boulders above them. He motioned for Kendall to come closer.

Kendall recognized the yellow and black markings of the serpent, which was about three feet in length. He let out his breath slowly. "It's a rattlesnake," he mouthed silently.

Akish shrugged. "Yes, and so?"

"Those things are poisonous!"

Akish shook his head. "Not poisonous for a Snake Runner. That serpent has been waiting for you. He knows he must meet the rain gods. He will be your messenger."

Kendall's eyes met Akish's black ones.

The young man added, "The rattler sends the message of our need for rain to the gods. And you, K'en'dl, his captor, bring a message from the gods."

Hot chills ran down Kendall's back. This prophesied message was one he didn't know himself. "You're positive I won't get bit by that rattler?"

The snake raised its head sleepily, aware of their voices changing the shape of the air. Immediately, the tail lifted and shook, sounding like pebbles in a can.

"No one has ever died from a rattlesnake bite during the snake ceremonies," Akish assured him, touching his chest. "The gods know who has a good heart, and they tell the snakes. The serpents become tame in our hands and willing to help beckon the rain. But most important, K'en'dl, do not show fear."

Kendall's hands turned clammy as he began to climb up to the higher ledge. Rocks skittered under his feet. The rattlesnake's body twitched, and the head shot up, tongue flicking. Its tail shook eerily in the quiet air.

Reaching the smooth boulder, Kendall was face to face with the reptile. Perspiration dribbled down his face and neck. The snake didn't move. The reptile seemed to study the eagle feathers fluttering on top of Kendall's head.

Kendall crouched, tense, alert. He couldn't do this. He was petrified. His stomach churned. Kendall was certain he would throw up any second.

Akish slowly rose to his feet, and Kendall knew he was watching him from below. Kendall wondered if maybe the young man was testing him by pushing him toward a rattlesnake, but he didn't think so. This was his own personal test. Was he pure enough to bring the snake back for the ceremony? Were his own prayers worthy of the Snake Clan? These days of the snake ceremonies would prove it. Not only to Akish and the others, but most of all to himself. He was here. Now was the time.

"Never pick up a coiled snake," Akish whispered from below. "Use your feathers."

Kendall pulled the bundle of eagle feathers from his sash. He held it out and waved it over the rattlesnake. The dancing feathers caught the snake's eye, and after a few moments, the serpent seemed to relax and began to unwind its coiled body. Kendall continued to stroke the rattler with the eagle whip. Salty sweat trickled into his eyes. Do it, he told himself.

Swiftly, before he could lose his nerve, Kendall copied the movements Akish had made to capture the bull snake. For a split second, his hand hovered in the air above the rattler, then he grabbed the rattlesnake behind the neck. With the other hand he caught the whipping tail and held it close to his chest. The snake couldn't move. At first the reptile wriggled against him, but Kendall stroked its body gently, his heart thumping wildly. After a moment the snake relaxed and began to rest in Kendall's arms.

"*Aaiiihh!!*" Akish yelled. He lifted the bull snake above his head and jumped down the slope to the valley floor.

Kendall let out a whoop of joy. He'd done it. He'd actually caught a rattlesnake. Holding the snake, he hollered the entire way back down the rocks.

Suddenly, from a mile farther north, they heard yells

echoing off the mountain ridges as another Snake Runner caught his sacred prey.

"We must run back without stopping," Akish said. "Be careful with your serpent, boy-man."

Kendall grinned back. "You, too. Race you back, future Snake Priest."

Akish appraised Kendall. Then he slowly smiled. "No, we won't race. We will run together."

Kendall put his rattler inside the snake bag and held it in the crook of his arm against his body. Then he and Akish ran the miles back over the empty desert to Sky City.

Hot wind flapped at the headdress as he ran. He had finished his water, and the empty deerskin pouch bumped lightly against his thigh. Brief clouds covered the sun, then moved out of the valley, a breeze kicking up dry dust.

Carrying the rattlesnake next to his heart as he ran was exhilarating. Fatigue disappeared with every mile. He let out another whoop of joy. Next to him, Akish laughed, and they yelled together as loud as they could.

Climbing the cliff to the village was also easier. When Kendall neared the summit, Akish reached out a hand and helped him over the top.

People lined the streets to watch the Snake Runners return with the setting sun, carrying their precious cargo. Little children and toddlers pressed against the walls of the houses when they saw the running, yelling, white-painted Snake Runners bringing armfuls of snakes right into the village. Mothers held them close, whispering in their ears and smiling. More snakes meant more rain.

There was a sudden hush as Kendall ran through the

streets back to the kiva. He knew people were whispering about him, the boy-man messenger. Then he realized they were pointing at his snake as he took it out of the bag to show. The Keresan word for rattlesnake was repeated over and over.

The men stood back as he entered the kiva. The dim, cool room went quiet. All eyes were on him. Kendall's rattler was the only one caught that day. Akish led him to a row of clay jars and Kendall helped the rattler slither into the pot. He sprinkled two pinches of yellow cornmeal in the jar for the snake's food.

"Your first snake of the day—the rattlesnake," Ogath the medicine man said. "You should be proud. Only the rattler knows who is the most pure."

The medicine man spread a layer of fine sand in a circle over the floor in front of the altar. Akish led Kendall to help form a circle around the altar with the other runners. They sat cross-legged, knees touching. After everyone was settled, the Snake Priests went to the clay pots and released the snakes in the middle of the circle.

A tangled mass of reptiles writhed on the floor before the altar. Kendall saw gopher snakes and bull snakes of every size and color. And there was his rattler right in the middle.

Prayers were offered over the snakes, then the singing began. Kendall felt soothed by the deep chanting sound of the men's voices as they sang together. Every sound and movement was done gently and slowly so as not to alarm the snakes. The singing stirred the animals, and they rolled together, playing in the sand.

A huge bull snake slithered toward the old man with his

eyes closed sitting next to Kendall. The reptile crept up the man's bare leg, yet the man never moved, never even twitched. A few moments later, the snake coiled itself in front of the man's breechcloth and went to sleep.

Kendall watched as one by one the different snakes chose a lap to curl up in and go to sleep. The old man ended up with four snakes coiled in his lap.

A moment of terror swept over Kendall as the yellow rattler eyed him. He tried to keep singing and not look into the reptile's eyes. He felt the rattler's tail touch the skin of his thigh and tried not to jerk. Slowly, the snake crept up his body, slithering from side to side over Kendall's toes, then across his knees. Listening to Kendall's soft singing, the rattlesnake coiled into a ball in the bowl of Kendall's leather apron and went to sleep.

CHAPTER

TEN

On the second day they ran west. Kendall captured two garter snakes that were tame and easy to carry. On the third day, he and Akish set out to the south as dawn washed across the ridge of mountains. And on the last day of snake gathering, the Snake Runners ran east facing the sacred *K'atzim'o* towering before them.

Kendall grew to love the hunt more each day, the taming of the wild snakes, running home with the reptiles cradled in his arms. His initial fear over handling them soon disappeared as his past life seemed to fade and he became a true Snake Runner with the other men of the clan. The whisperings throughout the village were that in no other year had so many snakes been brought from the desert. Excitement was in the air as the kiva filled with writhing, slithering reptiles.

Kendall felt as if he had gained the respect of his fellow Snake Clan runners as his rattlers and garter snakes curled up in his lap each evening for the singing, blessing, and entertainment of the snakes.

It was easy to forget about home, and it was also easy to forget about the shining metal strangers whom they hadn't seen for many weeks. Whenever thoughts about the bearded, armor-clad conquistadors came into his mind, Kendall wondered where they were and when they might be back, but in the midst of the snake ceremonies, it was easy to forget about them. Their valley was so isolated, the rest of the world faded away.

On the last night, the snakes were washed in sacred water and fed the finely ground cornmeal. The Snake Priests drew the final sand picture before the altar. Four borders of yellow, green, red, and white sand were created to make a frame. Inside this colorful frame, four circular clouds were drawn at the top of the picture. From each cloud a white zigzagged lightning bolt struck the earth. Black sand became raindrops falling from the sky.

Every day storm clouds entered the valley, hovering low and rumbling with thunder, but there was no rain yet. Whispers filled the kiva as the men wondered when the rain gods would finally release the rain.

"Let us concentrate on fulfilling our duties the gods gave us in the days of the ancients," the head Snake Priest said to the group assembled the final morning. "There are almost a hundred snakes in jars around the walls of this chamber. The promise of rain is upon us."

The old man who held several snakes in his lap every night smiled at Kendall. "Near the end of the snake ceremonies, the people are always worried. But there has never been a year when the rain gods did not bless us."

"Never?" Kendall asked.

The Snake Runner smiled again. "Never, boy-man."

The elderly man sounded just like Armando when he had assured Kendall that in the days of the snake running, there was always rain. It was one of the few things he'd told him about the sacred Snake Clan and their duties.

On the final morning, Kendall bathed with the bowl of water Jeneum and her mother brought him. They helped him wash his hair with foamy yellow yucca suds. With careful strokes, he and Akish drew white lightning bolts on their arms, legs, and chests. Last of all, Kendall placed his jewelry around his neck, ankles, and wrists and secured the headdress, the snake whip tucked neatly inside his sash.

The Antelope Clan had built a *kisi*, a shelter made of cottonwood boughs, at one end of the open square in the center of the village. Kendall helped carry the clay jars of snakes inside the shelter. In front of the *kisi* a cottonwood board had been laid over the hole to *Sipapu*, the place of emergence of the gods, the place his mother lived now.

After the snakes had been transferred, Akish said to Kendall, "Are you ready, Snake Runner?"

Kendall nodded. He felt heady with excitement, and his leg muscles tightened, waiting for the final climactic dance.

They filed out with the other snake dancers, walking in rows. Kendall watched the Snake chief lead the way, a huge man with powerful muscles and loose black hair hanging to his waist. He struck a majestic chord by his appearance alone. Someday, Kendall would be that kind of runner—that kind of Snake Priest.

Someone brushed his shoulder and Kendall glanced up, but no one was standing that close to him. A shiver ran down Kendall's spine, and he remembered that night on the desert when he'd seen his elderly great-grandfather running past him into the darkness, white hair flying. Armando was watching him now from the spirit world. Kendall could sense it. Armando would help him do this dance properly to win the approval of the gods.

The village watched, hushed, as the two lines of Snake clansmen circled the square. The only sound was the faint tremor of the rattles and anklets moving with each step. As each man passed the *kisi*, he paused to give a mighty stomp with his foot on the board that covered the hole of *Sipapu*.

Akish and Kendall were at the end of their line. Akish crashed his foot against the board to give his signal to the gods; then it was Kendall's turn. Kendall's eyes flickered upward, and he saw the old man from the kiva give him a look of assurance.

"The gods are in the earth below us," the old man said softly. "Waiting, listening."

Kendall stepped forward, raised his foot, and stomped hard on the board. The resonating sound was deep and powerful. Kendall had never heard anything like it before. Shivers ran down the lightning bolts along his arms, as if the paint symbols themselves were electrified.

Those resonating strikes on the board told the gods below that the mortals were carrying out their sacred duty of remembrance. Their life-giving snake god had not been forgotten.

As he moved away for the next man, Kendall was startled to hear an echo rise up from the earth. A sudden gust of wind whipped Kendall's long hair about his face, then died again. An instant later, thunder rumbled inside the black clouds to the west. Kendall knew he had been heard.

Four times they circled the *kisi*, and each Snake Runner pounded the board with his bare foot as he passed. Solmnly, the Antelope clansmen began to shake their gourd attles, swaying as they stood in a long line outward from he cottonwood shelter.

With each circle around the *kisi*, and each stomp on the oard, the excitement grew. The crowd pressed closer, anticipating what was going to happen next.

The drums pounded faster, harder, more furiously. The ound kept building until Kendall could feel the beat inside is body, vibrating his bones, his mind, and his heart with he steady pulse. Apprehension made him sweat. Something vas about to happen, and he didn't know what to expect.

Suddenly, the Snake chief kneeled in front of the *kisi*. Ie leaned inside, hidden for a moment by the branches and reenery. When he stood up again, Kendall felt perspiration rip down his back. His throat was dry.

A bull snake was in the man's mouth, its body held firmly etween his teeth. He grasped the reptile's head in one hand nd the tail in the other to keep it from squirming. His eyes vere black as night beneath his white paint. He nearly rinned at the crowd, holding his snake with his mouth.

The Snake chief moved around the circle of watching villagers, showing off his snake. A second man followed, olding the snake whip, stroking the snake with the feathrs to keep it calm and happy as they danced around the enter of the square.

Glancing up, Kendall spotted Jeneum standing on the oof of one of the houses, clustered with a group of women nd children. The breeze of the approaching storm lifted er hair and swirled long strands about her face. She brushed hem away, never taking her gaze from him.

Seeing her dark, soulful eyes, Kendall knew at that moment that his destiny was here. He belonged with Jeneum and her brother, Akish. This was more real to him than the trailer at home, more real now than Dad or Brett. That seemed crazy, as if his life back home were the unreal one, a distant dream. But he couldn't think about his old life. It hurt too much. He missed his father and brother, but he couldn't go back. Here at Acoma he could forget Juanita Lovato existed, or ever would in the future.

The magical power of the ancient dance seemed to fill Kendall's entire being as he watched the Snake Runners dance with their snakes. The magic was stronger, more filling, and more loving than ever before. Kendall didn't think he could give this up to return to a home with someone who didn't know or even care what this meant to him.

One by one, the snake dancers knelt in front of the *kisi*, picked up a snake in his mouth, and began the circling dance. At the end of each journey around the square, the snake was gently laid on the ground.

A snake gatherer stood watch to keep the reptiles from wandering into the crowd. When a dancer was finished dancing with his snake and laid it on the ground, the gatherer quickly scooped the serpent up over his arm before it could wriggle away. Soon the gatherer had a dozen snakes hanging like limp noodles over his arm. When his arms got too full, he placed them in a circle at the other end of the plaza.

The first time around the circle, Kendall guided Akish, delicately stroking the snake to keep it calm and soothed. When Akish was finished dancing with his snake, he directed Kendall to the *kisi*.

"Your turn, snake-boy," Akish said.

Kendall's heart thumped as he knelt on the ground. The yellow rattler stared at him from the mass of writhing snakes. Calmly, the reptile flicked its tongue as if it wanted to taste Kendall. Kendall got the distinct feeling the snake had been waiting for him. After all the nights of songs and caresses and sacred corn pollen, the snake knew him. A bond had been forged between them in a strange, magical way.

Kendall held the reptile gently in his mouth between his teeth and supported the snake's body against his naked chest. Akish followed, keeping the snake uncoiled with the soothing stroke of the whip.

Kendall's mind crowded with a thousand thoughts and fears. He didn't want to drop the snake. He didn't want to get bitten. Kendall knew he couldn't think those things. Impure thoughts would ruin the ceremony and tell the snake he wasn't worthy. A moment later, Kendall's heart suddenly calmed. He felt the presence of invisible Snake Clan spirits walking beside him.

Women and girls came forward dressed in their ceremonial dresses and jewelry. Carrying baskets of cornmeal, they threw the yellow pollen on the dancers as they circled with the snakes.

Jeneum was among the girls, and Kendall watched her moving in the soft robes of deerskin, embroidered in vibrant colors. She raised her eyes and lifted her hands, and Kendall felt a gentle shower of cornmeal fall over his head and shoulders, turning his arms yellow.

"Jeneum—" he started to say.

She put a finger to her lips and smiled.

When all the snakes had been danced with, the Snake

and Antelope chiefs knelt on the ground to draw. Out of the cornmeal appeared a picture of the six cardinal directions—west, south, east, north, zenith, and nadir—the heaven above and the earth below.

As soon as it was finished, the Antelope Priests carried the mass of snakes to the circle of cornmeal and gently placed the reptiles on top for a final blessing. The snakes turned yellow after being bathed with the fine cornmeal. The reptiles wriggled and writhed in a heap, entwining their long bodies together in knots.

When the blessings were completed, a signal was given for the final task, the most important one. Each Snake Runner gave a loud whoop and dashed to the circle. Scooping up armfuls of snakes, the runners headed for the cliff trail.

Holding his rattler, three garters, and a bull, Kendall ran for the edge of the cliff, following Akish, whose arms were also loaded with snakes.

Strangely, the snakes stayed calm, although their long bodies curled and uncurled across Kendall's shoulders as he carried them down the narrow footpath to the desert floor.

It was getting dark when he stopped running at the base of K'atzim'o. Bending over, Kendall freed his snakes to return to the four corners of the earth. In the dusk, he could see dozens of Snake clansmen spread in all directions over the valley, releasing their snakes. It was important that the message for rain be sent to the gods under the earth as quickly as possible.

Squatting in the rocky shale, Kendall watched his snakes zigzag across the sand. One by one, they silently disappeared around the boulders and rocks into the darkening twilight.

"I'm almost sorry to see them go," Kendall said.

Akish smiled. "You mourn your snakes like a true Snake Runner."

Bonfires had been lit along the cliff edges to light the way back for the runners. Kendall stopped to watch a mass of black clouds hovering over the towering mesa. Lightning streaked across the sky, crackling like fire. Stars and moon were completely hidden tonight.

"Drink this," Akish instructed Kendall when he reached the kiva. Kendall swallowed the bowl of herbs quickly, the same bitter brew he'd drunk at his initiation; then he and Akish stood at the cliff edge to retch.

"Get it all out," Akish told him. "Or your belly will swell up with the power of the clouds and burst."

With the back of his hand, Kendall wiped his mouth. And that's when he felt the first drops of warm rain. The patter of rainwater was soft, like someone shyly tapping him on the shoulder. Dark wet splotches stained the flat rock streets.

The raindrops grew stronger. Kendall tilted back his head and let the water run down his face, smearing the ceremonial paint. Soon his headdress feathers grew soggy.

After the final purification rites, Kendall left Akish in the kiva talking with Zoltan, his cousin-brother, and climbed the ladder to watch the rain and the rejoicing villagers dance around the sizzling fires. No one minded getting wet after the dry summer months.

Kendall wandered the darkened streets. The shells and rattles at his ankles made tiny tinkling noises. Under a flash of lightning, he was startled to see Jeneum running toward the path that led to the large water cistern below the cliffs.

Jeneum glanced back over her shoulder but didn't seem

to see Kendall. He couldn't help following her as she scrambled down the smooth rock slope. When she reached the
deep pools of clear water, the girl paused, raising her arms to
the wet sky, then turning in a slow circle like a dance.

Kendall crouched behind her, out in the open and watching, but the dark night made a good cover.

Suddenly, Jeneum whirled. "Who is there?" She sucked
in her breath when she recognized him under the lightning's flickering sparks.

He moved toward her. "I didn't mean to scare you. I saw
you come this way."

"I'm not scared," she said. "This is a beautiful place to be
in a storm. And it's been so long since we've had a good one."

She lifted her face and the heavens opened. Cool rain
poured from the sky. Then Jeneum looked at Kendall and
their eyes met. She beckoned with her hand. "Come with
me." She led Kendall down the slope, past the cistern, to an
overhang of rocks on the far side.

The rain became a waterfall pouring off the rocks above
them and running down into the cistern, filling it like a
swimming pool. The noise of thunder and lightning was
deafening, as the sky ripped open. Combined with the noise
of the waterfall, it was impossible to talk.

The snake ceremony was over, and the rain had come.
The spirits of the magic, past and present, crowded around
Kendall's heart. He wanted to yell and shout and weep all at
the same time.

He stood with Jeneum under the small cliff overhang,
crouching on the rocky surface behind the rushing down-
pour. Kendall could see her laughing. The sound of her

voice brushed his ear. She swept her tangled wet hair off her face. It was a mess clear down to her knees.

"You should have tied your hair back," he yelled above the waterfall.

"You still have paint on your face," she mouthed to him.

The painted lightning bolts on his arm dribbled in white rivulets. He grinned at her and stepped under the waterfall, letting it pour over him. Kendall rubbed his face and chest, and the last of the white and brownish red paint washed off, disappearing into the rocks.

Jeneum watched him from a kneeling position. Then Kendall reached over and grabbed her arm, pulling her under the water with him. She squealed with the shock of the pounding waterfall rushing over her head. The summer rain turned colder as the night aged.

Kendall tried to pull off the feather headdress, but the whole thing had knotted together with his own sodden hair. He could tell it was probably sticking up all over and looked ridiculous. Jeneum pointed at him, silently laughing, then covering her mouth.

He leaned closer. "You laugh at me—you get punishment."

"What are you going to do?" she dared.

Kendall ducked her under the strongest part of the waterfall, the sound of water roaring in his ears. Jeneum screamed and tried to grab his arms to pull him in as well, but he darted under the overhanging rocks.

She ran after him, trying to keep her balance, and they sat down together to catch their breath. It was as if they had just stepped out of a lake. Kendall watched her, water trickling down her cheeks, her long eyelashes stuck together.

"You did very well with your snakes and dancing," she told him.

"I thought you did good, too. With your cornmeal throwing, I mean." Kendall laughed at himself. How stupid that sounded.

She smiled as the pounding waterfall rushed over the rocks and fell into the cistern below.

"Your dress is ruined. I'm sorry I ducked you."

"It will dry," she said. "Just wait until I get you back."

She was quick. The next moment, Kendall found himself sprawled under the gushing waterfall, flat on his back. He laughed and got a mouthful, but didn't move. Just lay on the hard, curving boulders, arms wide, water splashing everywhere.

"Thank you," he yelled. "This feels wonderful."

"You would think so," she said, giggling again.

It was fun to make her laugh.

"I'd push you into the cistern and let you drown," Jeneum told him, "except you will contaminate the drinking water." Jeneum crouched behind him and pulled him back out of the flood. "Now sit up and I will fix your hair."

They sat behind the curtain of water while she began to untangle his hair. Her fingers were cold, but soft and expert as she knotted his hair at the nape of his neck, then braided it down the middle of his back.

"I don't have a decent comb," she said, "only fingers," and Kendall felt her warm breath against his neck.

When she finished, they traded positions, and Kendall repaired Jeneum's hair. He felt clumsy, and her hair was so thick it took him a long time to smooth out the long black strands.

The rain stopped beating the rocks and finally settled into a slow, steady rhythm. Jeneum rested her chin on her knees as Kendall finished braiding.

Jeneum suddenly pulled away. She put her hands over her face. "I am so stupid! The rain has made me crazy."

"What are you talking about?"

"We shouldn't be doing this," she whispered.

"Why?" Kendall asked. "What's wrong with what we're doing?"

Her black eyes stared at him like the dark bottomless cistern pools. "Sometimes, K'en'dl, you are Acoma, and sometimes you are not. Don't you know what fixing each other's hair means?"

Kendall shook his head slowly, wondering what they'd done wrong. Jeneum's face looked so alarmed.

She opened her mouth to speak, then stopped. "I can't even say it."

"Yes, you can. You can tell me. I won't say a word to anyone else. I promise."

"No, I can't," she cried, and got to her feet, hiding her face.

Kendall didn't know what to say. He couldn't even think what it was that would have her so worried. Or was she afraid of something?

"Jeneum, you don't have to be scared. I would never hurt you."

She just shook her head and turned to leave. "It's late. We'd better get home. Akish will be worrying."

He rose, then held out a hand to help her up from the rocks so they could begin the climb back to the village.

"Wait," she said.

He turned back.

"I've never said anything like this to a boy, or man, before." Jeneum spoke so softly Kendall had to duck his head to hear her. "K'en'dl, I hope you stay here at Acoma for a long time."

He reached for her hand, and she didn't pull away. "I'm not leaving," he told her. "My old life is no more."

Jeneum gazed into his face with surprise. "Surely there is a family who waits—your parents . . ."

Kendall looked out into the darkness beyond the shelter of the boulders. "My mother lives in the land of the dead."

Jeneum reached out to touch his face. "The loss of your mother is very sad for you. And your father?"

"I'm not sure he waits for me or my mother anymore. I know he doesn't. He has forgotten her already."

"But you can't forget."

Kendall shook his head. "She is alive here, she always will be. I can run here and fight to keep her alive."

Jeneum buried her face in his shoulder. Kendall had to stop himself from pressing his lips against her hair.

"I'm going to keep fighting to remember. To never forget. You help me remember, Jeneum."

She raised her face to look at him. "I'm glad, K'en'dl."

"I've already decided to stay, maybe forever."

CHAPTER
ELEVEN

Kendall stood in the fields with Akish, a wooden hoe in his hands, gray clouds a thick blanket overhead. They bent between the rows of corn, digging narrow irrigation ditches to channel the flooding water.

The mud was gooey paste, six inches deep. Kendall's bare feet sank as he tried to walk and work at the same time.

"I have never seen the gods give so much rain," Akish said. "It is running right off the top of the earth."

"Too many dry months, and now the ground cannot soak it in," Kendall said.

"For a new farmer you are learning well."

Seeds had been washed away, and the few green cornstalks were now flattened to the dirt, roots shifting in the soggy earth. Unable to take the relentless pounding from the skies, the small plants were in danger of being swept away.

"Did we gather too many snakes?" Kendall asked.

Akish grunted. "I don't know, boy-man. When the first god appeared to the ancients, he brought rain after years of drought. Rain is life. And he brought us life. I've heard stories of his healing, the miracles, and great knowledge. He also said that one day he would return."

Kendall looked up. "Is all this rain a sign of his return?"

Akish shrugged. "Only Tubaloth would know. When he

left, he returned to the Father Sun god, but he promised we would live with the gods after our life here is over."

"Just like the snakes," Kendall said, pausing to straighten his aching back. "They grow a new life each time they shed their skins."

"And their zigzag movement is the lightning that brings the rain," Akish added. "That's why our god was called a great serpent."

"My great-grandfather taught me some of this, but he died too soon."

"Losing the elders before they have passed on their knowledge is a true loss," Akish said. "That explains why you are so ignorant at times."

Kendall glanced up and saw that his clan brother was teasing him. He grinned, and they attacked their canals again, working together to shore up the plants and route the mud and water.

Sometimes it appeared hopeless. He and Akish had worked for days to stay the onslaught of torrential rain, running the miles back to Acoma when it grew dark.

While Kendall hoed row after row of struggling corn, he thought about his words to Jeneum the night under the waterfall. He meant what he'd said. He was staying. At least until the gods told him what to do. He had to have faith that when the time came, he would know the right conclusion to the powers that had brought him here. He'd spent so much time over all these weeks thinking about the decision. Weighing the pros and cons.

What was the magic doing to him? It seemed as though the powers in the universe caused the clock to stop. Time was standing still for him. He'd been given this chance to return to the time of the Snake Clan and learn the old ways. He couldn't help missing Dad, and he even missed Brett. It was almost inconceivable to think about never seeing them again. But how could he leave Jeneum and Akish and the life here? The decision felt like torture, a mental tug-of-war. Whatever he decided, he would be filled with heartache.

Since Armando's death and his initiation into the kiva, Kendall had felt out of place even with his own father and brother. He cringed thinking about the last time he'd seen his father—knocking him over in the living room and then running out the front door. He shouldn't have done that, and he wished he'd had a chance to make things right, but Dad and Brett were Anglo, and they didn't understand who he was. His blood was split bewteen an Anglo father and an Acoma mother, but he'd chosen to become Acoma. That's where his heart lay. Nothing could change that, even though he loved his father. The life here with Akish and his family was everything he wanted.

His father had chosen to marry Juanita, and it had been the right time to leave. The enchanted passageway was a gift from the gods. He'd been given a blessing to learn the ways and knowledge of the Snake Clan. But the ending to this gift was a mystery, and Kendall wasn't sure he even wanted to know what it was. It had now been months since they'd seen the steel-clad cavalry, but the threat of the conquistadors still lurked somewhere beyond the horizon. Nobody knew what was going to happen with those strangers from across the ocean.

Was Kendall meant to stay or go home? He wanted both

worlds, but he knew that was impossible. And the gods had been silent. It felt like his heart and mind would break in two trying to figure it out.

Early-morning runs to Enchanted Mesa were part of Kendall's daily routine, but he avoided the desert where the miniature mesa stood. The enchanted passageway was too powerful to get very close, so he stayed away.

Kendall became so immersed in his new life that he lost track of the passing season until the cottonwoods along the riverbed began to turn bright yellow and orange.

The days turned to hunting, skinning, and tanning hides before game became scarce. Jeneum traded pelts for salt from the Parrot Clan, and the last of the rabbit and deer meat was preserved and drying in the upper floors of their home.

Harvest time arrived, and Akish, as well as the other men, worried about the crops. The skies had gone dry. Not another drop fell. The growing season had seen either too much or too little rain to create a good harvest. Kendall helped pick the corn and beans and hauled baskets back and forth between the fields and the village, carrying them up the cliffs to place them in the storerooms. But it came to an end too quickly.

"What shall we do?" he asked one day as they turned the brown cornstalks under the soil for mulch for the winter.

"If we are frugal through the cold months," Akish said without looking up, "nobody will go hungry."

Kendall knew he was one more mouth to feed. Perhaps he *should* leave. Uncertainty as to what was the right decision was driving him crazy.

When he mentioned this to Jeneum as she kneeled at

her grinding, she shook her head. "No, you cannot leave," she said, but then her face flamed red and she lowered her eyes.

Kendall heard the catch in her throat and knew she was embarrassed at even saying those words to him. She jumped up from the floor, cornmeal powdering her face and arms, and ran up the ladder to the roof.

Ever since the night under the waterfall, Jeneum had seemed shy around him, and Kendall was afraid he had shamed her somehow. He knew they liked to be together, and it was easy to talk and laugh with her, but he still didn't know what had happened that night of the first storm.

To try to make it up to her, Kendall decided to make Jeneum a gift. He wanted her to have a necklace of blue turquoise that matched his own. He took his last rabbit kill to the Eagle Clan and bought a stone from the clan's jewelry maker. Kendall picked the prettiest teardrop shape in a deep blue, and the older man helped him fashion the stone and string it on a thin cord of leather.

After working the field on their final day before the frost began, Akish and Kendall ran back to the cliff village. As the village came into view, Kendall put out a hand to signal Akish to slow down.

Akish panted. "Are you ill?"

Kendall shook his head. "I need to ask you something."

"It must be serious."

Kendall caught his breath and began to walk. "On the night of the snake dance I found Jeneum at the cistern below the cliff."

Akish halted, staring at him. "Did you meet there for a purpose?"

"It was—just a coincidence. We ended up under the waterfall."

"And?" Akish prodded. "There must be a reason for you to tell me this."

"Something happened that made Jeneum embarrassed. She wouldn't tell me why."

Akish raised his eyebrows. "What did you do under the waterfall?"

It sounded so silly now, Kendall didn't know why he'd brought it up, but he had to know what he'd done to make Jeneum uncomfortable.

"We were soaked. We played in the water. We—we ended up fixing each other's hair. She combed and braided mine, then I did hers."

Akish stared at Kendall some more, then his face twitched into a smile. He shook his head and laughed. "You were playing children's games in the rain, and you ended up with something much more."

"I don't understand."

"Jeneum knows that only husbands and wives brush and fix each other's hair. And when young couples do that, it is a sign that they are engaged. They might even do it in public as a way to announce that they have promised themselves to each other."

Kendall sucked in his breath and bent over, then looked up at his Snake brother. "No wonder she wouldn't tell me. Is she worried that the whole village thinks we're engaged?"

Akish gave a slight shrug. "Did anyone see you?"

"No, it was dark and late and pouring rain."

"Then I would not worry about the rest of the village."

"What do I do?"

"Jeneum is probably uncertain what your relationship is," Akish said. "Since you have never courted or asked a formal proposal, she's modest enough to feel shy around you."

"Aren't we both pretty young to get married?" Kendall asked, trying not to show his surprise. Marriage was years away, wasn't it?

"Most people start getting married at about your age," Akish said. "Or within the next year or two."

"Why haven't you married yet, my Snake brother?" Then Kendall added jokingly, "Aren't you way past your years?"

Akish shook his head. "I must not marry until I know my mother and sister are cared for. It is a promise I made to my father."

"But your father—"

Akish shot his hand into the air, silencing Kendall. "I do not want to speak of the dead, boy-man. But promises are made to be kept."

That evening, Kendall paced the flat rooftop. A cold, clear desert sky sailed above, thousands of stars shimmering.

Jeneum suddenly appeared through the ladder hole. She gave a laugh. "K'en'dl, what is wrong with you tonight? You say nothing."

He stopped along the edge of the roof and grinned at her. "Just nervous." Kendall had never given a gift to a girl before. He wondered how to do it properly. He reached into his pouch, then took his hand out and let it drop to his side.

Jeneum came closer. "What are you nervous about?"

"Nothing. I mean—this." Kendall dug out the stone on its leather necklace and opened his palm to show Jeneum.

Under the yellow light of the crescent moon rising in the east, her eyes shone. She reached out to pick up the necklace, then turned it over and over in her hands, admiring the color, the texture, and the shape.

"Oh, K'en'dl, it is beautiful," she murmured. "And it is just like yours! It matches your own blue stone of the sky from your great-grandfather."

"Let me help you put it on."

Jeneum turned around and lifted her hair. Kendall took the leather cord and tied the ends together around her neck.

"I will wear it always. Until . . ."

Kendall looked at her. "Until what?"

"Until you tell me otherwise?" she said uncertainly. "You have given me a gift that I have accepted and love. Will there be more at my doorstep one day?"

Kendall touched the stone lying against her neck and smiled at her. "I hope to give you many gifts one day." It felt strange to think of a wedding and marriage. He wasn't ready yet. Neither was she. But he knew that it was easy to think of a future with her. Leaving Jeneum behind would be impossible.

"Perhaps when winter is over," Jeneum whispered.

Kendall thought about that. When the winter was over. After the winter he would know what he was supposed to do. The spirits would lead him to the answers by then. Perhaps he would go home. Or perhaps he would stay, living as a Snake clansman with his own people for the rest of his life. Surely, that's what he was meant to do. It felt like the right thing, and he'd never been happier—as long as he pushed thoughts of his father away.

"Mother, *Nai'ya*," Kendall whispered out loud to the heavens as he ran the early-morning miles to *K'atzim'o* the next day.. "If this is my destiny, you prepared me well. Did you know this all along?"

A tiny shaft of sunlight pierced the gray clouds.

"And you, Great-grandfather. You taught me the language and the runner's ways so that I could come here."

Naic Dia ocatc, Father Sun, bathed Kendall's face with warmth. His heart seemed to sing inside his chest as he smiled and ran with the magic of the enchanted valley. He loved his brother and his father, but they didn't belong here. They could never understand what Kendall had found in the past. He'd found his life, his dream, his purpose. The distance had become so deep and wide, Kendall wondered if he could ever cross it again to return. His life with his father seemed like a dream. A foreign place in a time that didn't seem to exist any longer. Everything here was more real, more alive somehow.

Dad and Brett would stay in the future without him. Perhaps forever. He knew that Juanita Lovato could never be a part of his life. She was a Spaniard and proud of ancestors who had tried to take Acoma away from *his* ancestors.

Kendall suddenly stopped in midflight. He bent over gasping for air. His ancestors. The Spaniards. A terrible feeling of dread squeezed Kendall's heart. His fate and future in the past of Acoma Valley suddenly took on a deeper meaning. He had no idea what year it was. How far into the future were the stories of the Spanish conquistadors and Acoma? He'd heard of battles and slavery, but when did they happen? Fifty years from now—or were his people on the brink of destruction right now? There was no calendar, no timekeeping except for the seasons and ceremonies that marked the year.

The gods were preparing him for some purpose, but Kendall had no idea what that purpose was.

CHAPTER
TWELVE

On the first day of snow, the shining metal strangers appeared outside the ridges of the valley. A weary runner from one of the tribes to the north had brought a warning.

Kendall and Akish stood huddled under blankets with the rest of the villagers as the messenger delivered the ominous news.

"The strangers' supplies have run low. Caravans of wagons have been rolling through each village. The metal men demand food to see them through the snows."

Someone murmured, "It is not our duty to make sure the strangers do not die."

"Tell them to return to where they came from," another voice spoke louder.

The discussion went on for the rest of that day as the *kahera*, the town crier, began calling from the rooftops for a meeting that very evening.

The chief of the Antelope Clan had the final word. "Let us remain peaceful as we always have. Give them blankets and a little food and they will leave us alone. Perhaps this will be the last time. We will pray that this is so."

The runner had a final message before the crowd dispersed. "My village was taken over, and my people are living outside in the cold. The strangers put their own women inside our homes and are using our storehouses of food and animals. But we are too few to fight, and everyone is too afraid to help us."

It was almost a challenge. The crowd's rumblings grew, and many men stepped forward to announce their willingness to fight.

One warrior said, "Let them come. We will show them that Acoma will never surrender. This is our home and they dare not try to take it from us."

Another shouted, "How can a few foreigners overthrow our rock fortress after we have lived here for more than a thousand years?"

The runner from the north said, "You have not seen their magical weapons. It is possible they will leave you alone out here on the desert by yourselves. But all the Big River villages have given up most of what they possess to remain peaceful."

He scanned the village perched on its rock citadel nearly four hundred feet in the air and nodded appraisingly. "You have the advantage of your envied rock home. They will find it difficult to reach the top. Their animals may be swift and strong, but the men are weak inside their metal clothing. They cannot run or climb or fight as we do."

"Their magical weapons do the work for them," a voice shouted.

Kendall heard laughter and cries of agreement.

The night was long as each kiva filled with clansmen discussed what should be done. The questions were hard and many. How should the strangers be greeted? Should their precious commodities of food be shared? If they gave the metal men food and supplies, would they leave permanently?

Or was it possible that if they told them they had no food, the strangers would give up and never return? It was difficult to know which course of action would bring the hoped-for results. The arguments on both sides were heated.

After visiting the kiva, Akish called a discussion of his own family in front of the hearth.

"If they are hungry, they will keep coming back until we give them what they want," Kendall said.

Akish rose in anger. "Our harvest was low. We will all starve if we give them our food."

"There will be enough," said Sharid quietly from the shadows. "The gods will provide if we are generous with others."

"I have counted our supplies and we have just enough," Akish began again.

Kendall swallowed. "Perhaps it is best if I leave so that I will not endanger your rations."

Jeneum gave a gasp. "No!"

Akish reached over and grasped Kendall's forearm. "I'm sorry, my Snake brother. I spoke in haste. It is unforgivable."

"I don't blame you," Kendall assured him. "We are all worried. I feel as though I am a burden to you. You didn't expect me here this cold season, and now the storehouses are especially low."

"You and I will run and continue to hunt this season," Akish said. "Perhaps we can lure a rabbit or fox from its nest. I won't let my family go hungry."

"Can we let others go hungry?" Jeneum asked softly.

Her mother agreed. "They say the strangers have now brought women and babies, too."

"So why don't their men hunt and farm for them?"

Akish's eyes blazed with frustration. "The strangers spent the growing season wandering hundreds of miles to the endless waters of the west. They look for more metal. But metal and gold do not fill hungry bellies. What stupid people!"

Sharid nodded. "You have spoken the truth, my son. Only a few men were left to farm, and they could not make anything grow. They do not have the seeds our mother, *Iatuk*, gave us. And they do not know how to ask the gods for rain."

"The strangers took over the fields of our northern neighbors, and there was no rain for them," Jeneum murmured. "The people were unable to perform the sacred ceremonies."

"It is a terrible thing not to please the gods," Sharid agreed, shaking her head.

Akish gazed into the flames. At last, he turned back to the circle they made around the hearth. "This will be the last time we give them food."

That night the nightmare came back. Kendall tossed and turned, then jolted straight up in bed. He gasped for breath and swallowed hard. Pushing back the blankets, he grabbed his legs, his feet, touching them, feeling them, making sure they were still attached, whole, and able to move.

Beside him, Akish slept soundly. Warm red coals from the sleeping fire lit the room with a soft glow.

Kendall flopped backward, sweat streaming down his face. A moment later, he sat up again, restless and anxious. Wrapping his arms around his legs, he flexed his toes again, then stared off into the shadows of the room. As he fingered his turquoise necklace, Kendall felt a strange uneasiness seep into the room.

In the morning a silent line of villagers stretched along the rock rim to watch the metal strangers ascend. At the base of the cliff, the Spaniards' horses were tied together, and two men remained to keep watch.

Kendall stood beside Akish and watched the slow ascent of the conquistadors up the narrow trail. The climb was accompanied by grunts and obvious cursing. Metal armor and swords clanged against the hard rock walls, and their helmets seemed to obstruct their vision, but the Spaniards didn't remove any of the heavy clothing.

Tomas, the interpreter, was with them again to ask the Acoma people for food. The small band of strangers walked down each narrow street, took the silently offered baskets of corn, turkeys, and blankets, and moved on to the next row of houses.

In a few hours, the collection was over, and discussions commenced in the open square between the village elders and the Spaniards, with Tomas interpreting.

"Why haven't they left?" Akish muttered as he and Kendall sat against the row of homes watching.

The village went deathly silent as three of the most senior elders knelt on the rock ground before the strangers. The metal strangers made them repeat words in the foreign tongue, words no one knew. A banner with a symbol of two intersecting straight lines rippled silently in the chilly breeze. A man cloaked in brown waved his hands in the air, pronouncing still more unfamiliar words.

"What is happening?" Akish whispered loudly.

Kendall recognized the symbol of the cross and the priest in his brown robe, but even he wasn't sure what ceremony was taking place.

A few minutes later, the strangers smiled under their helmets, looking happy as well as relieved. The village elders gave no indication of what they felt. Their faces were completely unreadable.

Tomas spoke words of thanks to the elders and told them they had made the right decision. Then the party of strangers returned down the steep path to their horses.

Word of what had occurred soon spread through the streets and rooftops. Kendall listened to the Antelope chief explain the ceremony. The elders had agreed to submit to the Spaniards and give them food whenever they needed it. The strangers had also insisted that the Acoma people learn about the strangers' religion. Their god had died on a cross of wood in a land far across the ocean. They said this god would save the Acomans' lives if they worshiped him and none else.

From his spot in the crowd, Akish laughed disdainfully. "How can this god save us if he cannot save himself from death? Our gods await us in the land of the spirits, where everyone is happy. Our gods have blessed us since the beginning of time if we are peaceful. Their god teaches them to steal and plunder."

Others in the square agreed with Akish, but the chief tried to explain. "By doing this, we have made a treaty of peace. We want peace above all. They have agreed to leave us alone, if we will provide food and listen to their teachings. It seems a small price to pay to be rid of them."

"But we're not really rid of them," a man named Cuomo said. "They will come back, if only to make us accept their god."

"We will listen respectfully," the elder Lehonti said, 'then refuse their teachings and go on with our own way of life."

The men around Kendall nodded again at the wise words, but some of the other men, especially the younger clansmen, grimaced at being made to bow allegiance to a nation they knew nothing about and didn't respect.

But after the metal strangers left, village life resumed.

Winter resumed also, getting colder, the snows deeper, the days shorter.

Jeneum and Sharid were frugal in their bread-making. Not a speck of corn was wasted. Every kernel was carefully ground and swept from their grinding stones into bowls.

Akish taught Kendall how to weave cloth. They also finished the tanning of fox, coyote, and rabbit skins. Together they sewed clothing, repaired tools, carved arrows, and restrung bows.

And every day they ran side by side through the valley to K'atzim'o.

"When we plant our seeds after the snow, we will be the fastest runners during the races," Akish told him one bitterly frigid day when they stopped to drink from their leather pouches.

Trickles of cold sweat ran down Kendall's brow. Running in these conditions made them hardy and strong. Each runner wanted to be the toughest, the most able to endure pain, and the swiftest of the village.

"We will win the sacred jar to plant in our fields so that we may have an abundant harvest next year," Akish added.

"We will eat all day and get fat."

Akish laughed, then placed a hand on Kendall's shoulder. "I'm glad you have come to share our home. It's good to run with you, Snake brother."

"There is no other place I would rather be," Kendall told him. "Acoma has performed a healing on my heart."

"Did you have wounds to cure?" Akish asked almost tenderly.

Unshed tears burned behind Kendall's eyes. He managed a brief nod. "I don't know if the wounds will ever be gone." He thought about his father and the hurtful way they had parted. Could he ever forgive him for marrying again? Dad marrying Juanita was wrong, a betrayal to his mother. His dad seemed so blind to it all. It didn't seem possible that his family could ever live peacefully. Kendall felt like he would hate Juanita for the rest of his life.

Akish looked Kendall in the eye. "You must tell me more of your life before you came here."

"Someday," Kendall agreed. "Someday you will know everything."

Near the longest night of the winter, the strangers appeared once more.

A small band of men approached, climbing awkwardly up the cliff trails and heaving themselves over the edge with packs and guns holstered at their sides.

Those swords and long-barreled guns inspired dread as well as awe, and Kendall could not stop thinking about what those guns could do to the bare, unprotected bodies of the warriors.

He recognized the leader from one of the previous visits. A tall man with chestnut-brown hair and a straggly beard led the way through the narrow streets. When the group reached the middle of the village, the talks with the elders began once more.

The Spaniards were on their way to the west and needed provisions. Could they have ground cornmeal instead of baskets of ears? They had no means to grind the corn, nor time. They offered to trade beads and trinkets for payment.

Most of the village stayed indoors by the fires. It was too cold to come out and watch. And no one volunteered to part with the small stores of food left in their houses. There were still too many months of winter left.

Akish spat on the ground. "Useless beads don't feed an empty belly."

Kendall pulled the blanket tighter around his shoulders.

The soldiers continued to demand help. They would wait patiently for the women to grind the corn and return tomorrow. The elders finally relented and asked if any women would grind corn. When Kendall and Akish returned home, Jeneum told her brother that she and a few other girls had agreed to grind.

"Are you crazy?" Akish exploded.

"Maybe I am," Jeneum answered. "But I cannot let another person starve."

"You could hardly call them people," her brother muttered.

All day, while Akish sat at the loom weaving and Kendall carved prayer sticks, Jeneum, Sharid, and two of their women neighbors worked on their knees before the grinding stones.

The first woman scraped the red and yellow kernels off the cob and did the first grinding with a coarse stone. The next woman ground it into a choppy mixture. During the third round, it was scraped into the stone bowl and ground still finer with a smooth pestle. The last woman made the cornmeal as fine and powdery as silk.

While they worked, the women sang their grinding songs. It was not a happy task, but the time and work seemed lighter when they sang, even though hearts were subdued about the soldiers who would receive it.

Kendall loved to listen to them. The melodies were soothing like a lullaby, the words asking the gods to help them in their work. He had often heard the grinding songs around the village during the summer as women worked outdoors in the shade. After the days of grinding, the baking began. Steamy hours in front of the outdoor ovens, where hot fires were burned, coals were removed, loaves of bread were slid inside, and the stone coverings sealed for baking. Kendall wished for those summer days again. Before the worry of the metal strangers had become so heavy.

The strangers camped below the cliffs that night. Light flickered from their campfires. In the stillness of the night, Kendall could hear their talk and laughter. He could even discern the horses' low rumblings in a makeshift corral where they were tied.

Lying on his stomach at the cliff's edge, Kendall glanced over at Akish, a shadow against the dark, somber night. They had been watching the strangers below the cliffs for more than an hour. "Let's go home. It's freezing."

"Why do I feel so uneasy when they are here?" Akish said. "I do not trust these strangers."

"There is a sense of trouble whenever they are near," Kendall agreed.

His Snake brother leaned farther over the cliff. "How barbaric they are. They must bathe rarely, for they smell just like the dung of the animals they ride. What good can it be to wear metal over their bodies? How they managed to cross a great ocean and travel across the southern desert is hard to fathom. That desert wasteland usually leaves no survivors."

"Think of what our arrows would do against their metal skin," Kendall said. "Our weapons would bounce right off without a mark."

"Someday they will want more than just cornmeal," Akish predicted.

"We must be careful not to upset them," Kendall said, thinking how lame that sounded. How could he begin to tell Akish that these men were just the first of thousands of people from all over Europe who would explode across the entire continent?

CHAPTER
THIRTEEN

In the morning, there was not enough cornmeal to appease the soldiers. More was begged with promises of payment. The women of the village ground for another day, while the soldiers grew impatient to be on their way to the western mountains. They had heard there was gold to be found there.

Tomas stood in the center of the group. "They are going on a long journey and need much food to sustain them."

"Let them eat cactus," Kendall heard a voice call out. "We will not take from our own children any longer."

Kendall felt sorry for Jeneum and Sharid and the other women. They had been on their knees for so many hours grinding. Their compassion toward the Spaniards made him proud yet sad at the same time. The strangers' constant demands were making him angry. Everyone was tense and resentful. Thoughts of Juanita Lovato kept rising in his mind. Kendall pictured her sitting at the kitchen table—all those words of boasting for her Spanish ancestors.

Was there anything he could do to stop the past? It was a history that he alone knew, and even his knowledge was vague. He wondered if it was as bad as the stories he'd heard. The people hoped that the metal strangers would leave them alone after the winter was over. But Kendall knew that they wouldn't leave. The story had only begun.

"What is it, K'en'dl?" Akish asked as the men returned to their homes to wait.

Kendall shook his head and turned away. He didn't know what he was supposed to do. Tell the people to fight, to flee, or to submit to the demands? He didn't know which would be the best decision. Perhaps it was time to go back and talk to Tubaloth again. Kendall didn't know if he should try to visit the ancient medicine woman uninvited. He was young and male and basically a stranger to her. When he asked, Akish advised, "Tubaloth will summon you. Wait for the right time."

The only cure for Kendall's restlessness was running. Nobody ventured down the cliff with the strangers camped below, but Kendall stole down one of the back trails and ran the length of the valley until he was so exhausted he couldn't think anymore.

On the third day, the Spaniards' leader lined up his soldiers in the open square, commanding them to stand at attention and not move or disturb the inhabitants of the village. Since they were traveling, the soldiers did not wear the complete suit of metal armor, and they looked more like ordinary men. In fact, Kendall thought they looked uneasy, standing in their small group among so many unsmiling Acomans engulfed in robes of skin.

The pale sun moved slowly across the sky. The girls no longer sang at their grinding but hurried to finish the task. Everyone was eager for the strangers to leave, and tension boiled beneath the surface of the village.

At dusk, the soldiers dispersed through the streets to gather the baskets of flour and corn. Kendall stood next to Akish, watching them collect from as many houses as they could. Meager baskets were handed through the rooftops, and more than once the soldiers expressed displeasure at such pitiful offerings.

Finally, the group went down a second street and disappeared from view. Long minutes passed. Akish paced the narrow village road more and more feverishly.

"Something is not right," Akish finally said. "I am going to get my bow." He started up the ladder.

"Please don't get it yet," Kendall said, leaping up the ladder to restrain him. "If we look as though we're going to attack, the strangers may get nervous and pull out their guns. I'm sure they will leave soon."

A muscle in Akish's jaw twitched as he listened. "I will not fight, but I will be prepared."

Suddenly, there were shouts and cries from down the row of homes. Akish and Kendall hurried down the outside ladder to the street. Icy wind bit into Kendall's shoulders, his robe of rabbit skin falling down his back.

When they reached the homes of the Sun Clan, chaos had broken out. Several soldiers, their long-handled guns waving in the air, shouted at the throng of villagers.

"¡Por casualidad!" one of the soldiers cried, red in the face. "¡Por casualidad!"

Suddenly, Tomas ran past Kendall. "An accident, an accident," he shouted, seeming not to know what had happened but quickly guessing the meaning of the Spanish words.

Clan families poured from their ladders on the rooftops, joining the crowd on the street.

Kendall pressed closer, trying to see what had happened. He felt Akish pushing on his heels.

Inside the crowded circle the villagers fell silent. An old woman was lying on the ground, her eyes half-closed, a gash from her head oozing blood down the side of her face. Her hands lay still. A squawking turkey ruffled its feathers and tried to waddle away. One of the men grabbed it by the neck and picked it up.

A young woman kneeled on the rock beside the old woman, tears falling down her face. She tried to lift the old woman's body but couldn't seem to revive her. Wailing, she buried her face into the old woman's breast.

A ripple went through the crowd. "They killed her—the old grandmother is dead!"

Kendall felt like he'd been hit in the stomach. This couldn't be happening. But the blood was real, and the old woman lay unmoving on the ground.

The Sun clansman, the woman's brother, held the bird up in the air and his face looked terrible. "She was killed over a turkey! Look, her blood has even stained the feathers."

The crowd grew larger and noisier as word of the woman's death spread quickly.

In the confusion, the three soldiers who had been collecting food tried to leave, but Sun Clan warriors quickly surrounded them, stopping their departure. Within moments, without speaking or discussion, the warriors gathered rocks and began to throw them at the Spaniards.

Kendall caught Akish's arm as the young man struggled forward through the crowd. "Stop!" he yelled. "We need to find out what happened first. It must be an accident."

Akish pulled his arm away. "I will not stop. It has gone too far, killing a woman over a stupid fowl. There must be justice for this murder."

Glancing back to the street, Kendall saw the woman's family continue to throw stones at the soldiers. One by one, the Spaniards collapsed to the ground, arms up to protect their faces as the hail of stones grew heavier, pelting their bodies. Within minutes, the men were cut and bloody. Kendall turned away, sick. The Acomans were fighting back, the anger that had been building for months suddenly exploding into rage. How could everything get so crazy all at once?

The shouts of fighting reached the square, and the remaining ten soldiers stormed around the corner of the last row of houses, marching rapidly, weapons lifted and ready.

At the sight of the soldiers, the women screamed and began running in a panic down the street. Within moments, shots of bright yellow blasted from the barrels of the soldiers' guns.

A Bear clansman fell dead in the front of the crowd.

"Ah-a-a-a Ai'!" Akish yelled the war cry behind Kendall, and before Kendall could move to stop him, the young man withdrew an arrow from his quiver. Swiftly, he placed the shaft in his bow and pulled the string.

"Wait!" Kendall cried, but Akish and the other warriors ran to meet the oncoming soldiers.

The soldiers halted and held steady, firing still more shots from their pistols. Another Acoma man fell dead midstride, but the number of warriors was too great for the few remaining soldiers. As the warriors raced forward, the soldiers quickly retreated, fleeing to the edge of the village. Three made it over the edge and down the cliff path.

The rest of the Spaniards, including the leader, scattered through the streets, searching desperately for a means of escape. It didn't take long before they were surrounded. Kendall saw a soldier fall to his knees in front of a bare-chested Acoman. A torrent of Spanish poured from his mouth. The warrior raised his club and brought it down as hard as he could on the Spaniard's head, smashing the man to the earth in seconds.

The shock of the scene rooted Kendall to the earth. Cold no longer mattered. His stomach turned and bile bubbled up in his throat. He spotted Akish through the confusion and tried to push through the mob. Before Kendall could reach him, however, Akish let fly with one of his arrows, and the weapon found its mark, piercing a soldier in the breast just above his armor. The man collapsed onto his stomach.

The entire fight was over in minutes. More than a dozen bodies lay in pools of blood along the streets. The sinking sun dropped below the edge of the earth as Akish staggered over to Kendall. The young man was blood-spattered, a gash on his arm.

"Are you badly hurt?" Kendall asked.

Akish shook his head. "Help us drag the bodies and throw them over the cliffs."

The evening twilight was eerie and the mood somber. Kendall stood with the other men at the cliff's edge. He was glad it was nearly dark. He didn't think he could have watched the dead bodies, after being hurled over the cliffs, land on the desert below to be eaten by animals. It was a gruesome job, but many of the other men had been wounded and were already being taken back to their homes to be tended and given the healing herbs.

There was little sleep that night. Kendall sat in the corner while Jeneum and her mother helped Akish clean the dirt and blood from his wound, which wasn't deep. They bandaged it, and then Sharid washed her son's hair with yucca suds in a bowl of water. Jeneum fixed soup and bread, and they ate in a circle of silence, picking at the food.

Akish laid down his bowl, getting up to lay another branch on the fire. "Now they will leave us alone. They know we are too strong."

Kendall hoped he was right. But whispers filtered through the village. The three soldiers who had managed to get down the cliffs had escaped on their great galloping beasts. It wouldn't be long before they reached the northern fort and told the other metal strangers of the battle.

Today had been a small victory for Acoma, but there were more soldiers to the north. So many more. They would come back and bring their magical fiery weapons. Acoma had to be ready.

CHAPTER
FOURTEEN

Rituals for cleansing the village of death spirits were performed over the next few days. Afterward, Kendall noticed that Akish withdrew from the family, running by himself for many days. Fear of the future coiled like a poisonous serpent inside Kendall's belly as they all watched and waited.

It was still dark one morning when Kendall woke to hear the rustling of Akish's dressing by the fire. He slipped out from under the blankets and hurried to put on his own clothing. Akish was already up the ladder as Kendall jammed his feet into his moccasins and flew after him, taking the rungs two at a time. But Akish either didn't hear him or was ignoring him.

Three miles later, Kendall caught up to his Snake brother at *K'atzim'o* in the rugged boulders and rough shale.

Anger crossed Akish's face, and his breath came in spurts. "Go away, boy-man. I don't want to talk to you."

Kendall stared back. "You are running like you are afraid of your own shadow."

It was the wrong thing to say. The young warrior lunged at Kendall, and they fell to the rocks, wrestling like bullies on a playground. Akish managed to pin Kendall and sat on top of his legs.

"I do not run like a coward," Akish said, jabbing a finger at Kendall's chest. "I do not fear you. I do not fear the strangers. And most of all, I do not fear death."

"I'm sorry," Kendall said. "I never meant to call you a coward." He stopped struggling and Akish finally rolled off him.

They sat there as they had so many times over the months, but the serenity they'd always felt, the peace and happiness of their brotherhood, was gone. Stolen by the metal strangers. Fear of the future lurked throughout the village, creeping into every ritual, every song, and every meal.

"Akish, you are one of the bravest men I know," Kendall told him. "But there is something wrong inside of you. I can see it. I can feel it."

"It is not cowardice in my heart," Akish said quietly.

"What is it? Tell me what makes you run like a crazy man every day."

"I am trying to face myself, K'en'dl. I have now killed another man. An enemy, it is true, but I have taken a life, and I do not glory in it. Will a woman ever want a killer for a husband?"

"You didn't kill for pleasure," Kendall said. "You killed defending your home."

"Defending my home is the excuse I can give everyone, but I killed because I felt such rage and hate. I want to see the strangers dead. All of them."

"They should never have come," Kendall said quietly. "They should find their own spot of land and leave the villages in peace."

Wishing for that was only a stupid form of hope. A hope that wasn't founded on reality. He knew what was going to happen; he had been burying it deep in his memories. Kendall had hoped the stories were only myths of the future—stories embellished with the passing of time. But after the first battle a few weeks ago, he knew the tales were true. This was only the beginning. The worst was yet to come.

"Do you know what I really fear?" Akish said, turning to Kendall.

Kendall shook his head, his own nightmares still haunting him.

"I fear that the strangers will steal our fortress home and will force us out. I dread the last time I may run freely through our valley. I cannot fathom a future of never teaching my sons the Snake Clan ways—how to be pure in heart and become fearless Snake Runners."

"These things will never come to an end," Kendall told him. "They have been here since the beginning of time— how could they ever stop? You should not worry." He felt his face burn in the bitter cold sunrise. What a liar he was.

Why couldn't he tell Akish the truth? But he already knew the answer to that question. It was because of the nightmares. That evil presence that turned him ill, the fear that his feet were gone, that he would never run again. He couldn't tell Akish the truth because he couldn't face it himself. Whenever the nightmare visited him during his sleep, he pushed it away later. Kendall wanted to forget about it, hoping the dream held no meaning, no message, no truth.

"You are wrong, boy-man," Akish said abruptly, standing up.

Kendall looked up, startled.

"The medicine men have seen the future in their glass bowls. Last night in the kiva they prophesied the doom of Acoma. I heard them myself."

Kendall knew he couldn't contradict Akish's words.

Kendall might be the last Snake clansman of the future, but that didn't matter anymore. If he stayed, perhaps there would be no death of his clan and the runners. That must be the reason he was here—to save his own clan. It was too late to go back home. Too much time had passed. So many months. He would do whatever he could to save the future—to keep his Snake brother from suffering death at the Spaniards' hands.

The winter solstice ceremonies were held during the darkest part of winter. Fear cast a shadow over the ceremonies, and once they were finished, preparations to meet the strangers in war began in earnest. Days were short and frenzied; no one had any idea when an army would march into their valley.

Huge quantities of arrows were carved of obsidian stone and filed so sharp they drew blood at the slightest pressure. Knives and axes were sharpened, bows restrung, dozens of clubs cut and fashioned from tree limbs. Children gathered rocks and piled them in tall mounds along the cliff edges.

Zoltan, Akish's cousin, rose to speak in the kiva one evening as the men gathered during the cold winter night. "Why do we make such huge preparations for war? We are not warriors—we are farmers. Let us plead forgiveness from the strangers for the death of their leaders. We must make peace. For us and for our children."

Sitting next to Akish, Kendall could feel the young man's agitation. He glanced over, trying to warn silence with his eyes.

Ogath stood next to the altar. "It is true we have never

caused war with another tribe and have lived here peacefully since *Iatuk* brought us to this sacred spot. But we cannot forget that an innocent woman died in a squabble over a turkey."

Akish leaped to his feet, unable to contain himself. "More than an old woman died. We might have killed thirteen of these strangers from across the sea, but some of our own warriors died also, defending her death."

Zoltan nodded. "We evened the score that day. Perhaps our preparations are for naught. We have shown them that they have encountered a foe too formidable, and they have left for good."

Gicombo, one of the older warriors, shook his head vigorously. "Have you forgotten their steel coats and swift steeds? Their weapons that shoot fire? These people are not common folk who will farm and tend flocks and live in peace. They are soldiers, part of an army, and they want our fortress. They desire us to live as they do and worship their gods."

"Gicombo is right!" Akish shouted, then lowered his head as his outburst echoed through the circular room. "We have to be prepared to fight," he continued, speaking in a tight voice. "If only to defend and keep our home safe for our children and grandchildren."

"It will only bring death and destruction," Zoltan pleaded. "I had a vision last night. . . ." His voice faltered, yet everyone knew what he meant.

"If we are prepared, we shall not fear," Akish declared. "Our mother, *Iatuk*, will be with us."

Kendall couldn't help feeling proud of Akish. His words

of bravery in the face of a conqueror, his unshakable faith in the gods who brought life and food and family were inspiring. His Snake brother seemed truly to have no fears.

Kendall suddenly thought about Brett. Close and yet very far away. Brett was his blood brother, and Akish was his Snake brother. He felt close to both of them, but one was here beside him, and one was a great distance through time, at the end of a journey Kendall did not want to make.

Talk of battles surrounded him. Seeing the death of the warriors, the soldiers being thrown over the cliff, had made his thoughts turn to his family. The closer the metal strangers came, the more he remembered about home. He thought about running through the cottonwoods along the riverbanks, visiting his mother's grave, riding in Dad's semi with him and reading the maps. Those were the good memories of the life that had been destroyed by Juanita Lovato's presence. The gods had sent him here to face the past, the Spaniards, the war that loomed on the horizon. Kendall suddenly felt angry, helpless. He was terrified. He needed to talk to someone—needed to talk to his father. But he couldn't. This was something he had to do alone. Why had the gods sent him here? What could he possibly do that would prevent Acoma's destruction?

Three days later, shining metal and galloping horses could be seen crossing the desert in a cloud of dust. The preparations for battle had been finished. The last of the prayers had been sung at the altar, the last of the songs danced.

Tension lay thick throughout the village. Children stopped

their play. Old men no longer sat on their roofs in the few hours of winter sun. Each stood before his ladder waiting, watchful. Little food was eaten. Dread filled every belly and heart.

"It is time," Akish said to Kendall.

Kendall couldn't eat his own breakfast as he watched Akish prepare the war paint. There was silence in the room as Kendall followed Akish in daubing on the black, red, and white paint. Thick stripes were spread over their arms, legs, and face. Jeneum sprinkled a tiny pinch of their blessed cornmeal around the perimeter of the house and over their heads to protect them.

"We will be safe, won't we?" she asked Kendall.

He smiled to reassure her, not wanting her to be afraid. No matter what happened, he would make sure Jeneum was safe, even if it meant dying himself. "We are so well prepared on top of our rock home, they cannot possibly overcome us. Our warriors are the better fighters, and we have spent weeks preparing. I only wish I was more experienced with a sword and spear."

"But you can outrun anyone," Jeneum said.

Kendall could only smile grimly. "I'll do my best."

"After the battle," Jeneum said softly, fingering the blue stone necklace at her throat, "I will meet you at the cistern on the south side across the chasm."

"I'll be there," Kendall promised. "If there is a battle. Nothing is certain. There is always hope."

Across the desert, the sound of war bugles rang out among the company of soldiers.

Jeneum gripped Kendall's arm. "They are coming!"

Sharid climbed down the ladder from the upstairs rooms. She appeared calm, but her eyes looked fearful.

Akish finished filling his quiver with arrows. He walked over to his mother and put an arm around her. "Keep the soup hot. We will be back soon. This battle, if it comes to that, will not last long."

The entire village poured from the roofs, rushing to the edge of the cliff to watch the approaching army.

There was silence from the people as they listened to the distant jangle of bells on the horses' reins. The horses looked as though they had been dressed in a blanket of iron as they trotted forward row after row, an armor-clad soldier upon each back.

The bugles blared again, the notes loud and clear in the morning air.

Kendall shivered at the martial sound. Did death lie just around the corner? His thudding heart hurt inside his chest. He knew that it would take only minutes to run across the desert and be safe inside the mesa's passageway, away from all this. But just thinking that felt like a betrayal. He couldn't leave Akish and Jeneum. Their fates were his fate. His purpose had not been revealed. And yet he felt fear like he'd never known before. The taste was harsh in his mouth.

The army advanced, and Kendall could see shining armor of the finest steel on each bearded man. Heavy shields hung from their shoulders. Some had lances with double heads. Other lance heads had been formed in the shape of a crescent. It was overwhelming to see this European army of a long-ago century getting closer, advancing without a moment's hesitation.

Would their own spears and arrows be powerful enough to stop such armor and sophisticated firearms? The Acomans had no protective clothing, only skins and moccasins sprinkled with sacred corn pollen. The carved animal fetishes deep inside their sacred bundles exhibited their faith in the gods' protection.

Kendall glanced at the faces of the warriors. These men were his neighbors, his people. They showed no fear.

The Spanish leader rode forward. He was a red-bearded man who looked much like the past leader, whose body now lay with his comrades under piles of rubble on the desert floor. The two men could have been brothers. The same nose, the same eyes. This man also had the same quality of armor and an oiled long-handled gun at his side.

The sun withdrew behind a cloud, and the people standing at the edge of the cliff shivered against the frosty sweep of air.

Akish spoke next to Kendall. "I have counted them. Only seventy soldiers against hundreds of our warriors. They make me want to laugh. They cannot possibly scale our walls and fight us. We are more than ten times as many."

"But look at their weapons and the shields of steel."

Akish's fingers dug into Kendall's flesh. "Never doubt, boy-man. Never."

The leaders of each clan raised their clubs and spears to the sky, opening their mouths to release terrible yells and howls. Hundreds of Acoma men, along with the women and the older children, began to howl and cry their war yells.

Down below, the horses shuffled and pranced, obviously spooked by the deafening war whoops. The leader's horse whinnied and reared. The man reined in his steed, placing a hand on the animal's neck to calm it and trying to stay in the saddle at the same time.

Yelling along with his Snake brothers, Kendall watched irritation flash across the man's face. The Acoma warriors stopped as abruptly as they had started, but the war cries had the intended effect on the army below. The echoing silence was eerie, and the group of soldiers looked up at the impassive rock, clearly unsettled.

The Spanish leader raised his sword and wheeled his horse around, barking orders. The interpreter, Tomas, was brought forward to shout his messages up to the rock's inhabitants. Kendall watched Tomas cup his hands to his mouth, and his voice carried thinly up the sides of the cliff.

"I am General Vicente de Zaldivar. I have come from the capital, San Juan, as the commanding officer of our great expedition leader, Don Juan de Oñate. We are servants of the noble king of Spain, who now claims this land of Nuevo México. We have come in peace, Acomans." Tomas continued to shout, "We do not want to make war with you. But amends need to be made for the murders of our fellow comrades."

This plea for peace was met with stony silence. If war was not on their minds, then why had such a well-outfitted battalion come so many miles across the desert?

Tomas and the leader, along with two other men, conferred. Then Tomas stepped forward again and yelled, "Bring forth the men who murdered Maese de Campo Juan de Zaldivar and his fine soldiers. We have come to secure these felons and take them back to San Juan for trial. The rest of you can go on with your lives in peace."

Akish snorted in Kendall's ear. "We all participated, you fool. In defense of an old woman and the fowl that was stolen from her. Must we all die for defending a woman's honor?"

Zoltan stood on the edge of the cliff and stared down at the soldiers. "Does he expect us to turn our brothers over to him? If we release any of our fellow clansmen, we know we will never see them again."

General Zaldivar shouted further instructions to Tomas. "You must turn over these criminals! They will be given a fair trial and punished according to their crimes. Now come forward and show no cowardice."

At these words, the howls and yells began again on top of the cliff.

The leader kneed his horse, trotting forward with several men, whom he directed to ascend the narrow rock trail.

As the soldiers began to climb, the elder Gicombo gave a signal with his hand, and the youngsters of the village proceeded to rain stones down on them. The Spaniards tried to let the rocks bounce off their armor and keep going, but it became clear that they could not climb with such a torrent. They soon realized, too, that the path had been blocked with other large boulders. It was impossible to scale.

The group returned to the general in failure. Zaldivar galloped his horse back to the rear ranks, yanking the animal in a circle, then forward again, his agitation clearly rising. More orders were given, then the army broke apart and began to make camp for the night.

That night sentinels were posted at every path as well as behind the cliff embankment. The rest of the villagers returned to their homes. There was celebrating in the homes and kivas.

"The strangers' army has seen that they are no match for us," Akish told his mother and sister when he and Kendall returned. "They have decided not to attack."

Jeneum rushed forward when Kendall descended the ladder. "You are both safe," she said with relief.

Sharid was ready with food. After they ate, Kendall and Akish joined the other warriors in the kiva to rejoice over the initial victory.

But in the head kiva, plans were also made for the next day's possible battle. Captains over groups of men were appointed. The first group would advance, and if reinforcements were needed, more waves of warriors would be ready. The younger males would not fight. They would stay in the village and protect the women and children.

After the meeting was over and they were back at home, Kendall tried to protest his staying in the village, but Akish would not listen.

"We will all fight better knowing our women and children are protected by you and the other boy-men," Akish said. "You have not learned the fighting techniques or been endowed with the powers that come with the warrior-society initiation. But someday your turn will come. Especially," he added, "if these strangers persist in staying in our land."

"You might fall into the hands of the enemy without a brother to help you."

"But you are a most wondrous runner, K'en'dl. I trust

that, if necessary, you will take my sister and mother and know how to hide them."

Jeneum picked up the clay water jug to go to the cistern. "If a battle begins and you need to go closer to the edge of the village, meet me at the waterfall afterward so that I will know you are safe."

"Nothing will keep me from coming to you."

"I will pray to the gods for your safety."

In the morning, the cliffs crowded with villagers. Smoke could be seen from the soldiers' campfires, and the smells of cooking food drifted on the air.

Soon the Spanish troops were outfitted and standing at attention in perfect rows, awaiting their orders, lances at the ready, horses pawing the ground.

Tomas came forward again to yell up at the cliffs. "This is your last chance to surrender the criminals hiding among you. Surrender them or face death."

Laughter and jeering roared down at the soldiers.

"They are not going to give up, are they?" Akish said, amused.

When there was quiet again, Gicombo, the Acoma general, shouted down the cliff. "We will never surrender or give up our brothers, who acted in self-defense."

"Give them to us," Tomas repeated.

"Never," shouted Gicombo.

General Zaldivar quickly mounted his horse, his fury barely concealed. He galloped to the foot of the cliff and announced, "Be warned as of this moment. We will attack you now in full battle. Prepare yourselves."

Kendall could hardly believe his eyes when he saw the small Spanish army march to the second mesa on the far south side of the chasm and begin to scale the rock.

He retreated to the rear ranks to watch with the other male youth. The warriors talked among themselves. Nobody seemed to really believe the strangers would actually attack. Hundreds of Acoma warriors against seventy soldiers. Didn't the strangers realize they were outnumbered?

It wasn't long before the army reached the top. Kendall leaned over the cliff, his gut twisting to see the Spaniards so close with their armor and weapons.

Farther down the cliff edge, bloodcurdling whoops and war cries came from the Acoma warriors as they let loose an assault of stones and arrows across the chasm. The arrows and rocks hit their intended targets but immediately bounced off the metal armor and shields. Undaunted, the warriors kept up the barrage of arrows, but it seemed futile. Few found a good mark to cause any damage. Within minutes, even amid the onslaught of arrows, the strangers had loaded their guns with powder and balls.

"*¡Fuego!*" came the command.

A deafening blast shot from the guns, and the entire first wave of Acoma warriors was laid to the ground. Screams of agony punctured the air.

The men's shrieks brought the women rushing into the streets. Kendall and the other boys held them back and urged them to remain in their homes. Surely, this would be over soon.

A group of twelve Spaniards suddenly climbed over the edge of the cliff near the village. They had secretly scaled he massive rock while the main body of the army had openly attacked on the south mesa. Terror gripped Kendall's heart, but a group of warriors guarding the cliff edge poured forth a shower of clubs, stones, and arrows.

A shot rang out from one of the pistols, and Kendall saw an Acoma man keel over. Two more Spaniards managed to finish climbing the walls and opened fire with their guns. Several warriors charged to the scene to help their fellow clansmen but suddenly dropped to the earth as the bullets found their marks.

The Spaniards fired another volley, and more than a dozen warriors joined their brethren on the sacred earth of Acoma.

More warriors rushed forward, spears and hatchets raised. They fought hand to hand with the soldiers, clubbing with rocks and sharpened hatchets.

Kendall couldn't stop himself from searching for Akish. When he reached him, his Snake brother looked stunned and was waiting for orders from Gicombo. "No matter what we send," the young man said, "even a deluge of our rocks and arrows, it does not hurt them."

"They must be enchanted," Zoltan agreed. "It is impossible to hurt them."

Kendall shouted at him, "They're not magic! Look at the coats of steel that protect them. We have nothing like that. Our bare bodies are exposed and vulnerable."

Zoltan shook his head. "We have never had such a fight before. They look like men as we are, they live as we do. Perhaps these strangers really are gods."

"They are not gods," Kendall said fiercely. "They are only men and will bleed just as you do."

Akish turned to Kendall in frustration. "But they hav
magical weapons that pour fire without flint. Without fue
It is truly a miracle."

The fighting went on all afternoon until dusk bega
to creep over the horizon. Wave after wave of warriors trie
to engage the Spaniards in man-to-man fighting, but th
strangers' protective armor prevented any injury. Yet th
never-ending supply of guns and powder killed Acomans b
the dozen.

Finally, it was dark and the warriors retreated to thei
homes, dragging their dead with them. Across the chasn
the Spanish soldiers stayed on top of the rock and mad
camp without returning to the desert floor.

Kendall found Jeneum waiting at the cistern.

She kissed his hands and held her head to his chest. "
heard the thunder the strangers make. I can smell the burn
ing. What is it?"

"They have weapons that fire and kill instantly," Kenda
said, collapsing to one of the smooth boulders at the water'
edge. "But the warriors are brave and fighting a good fight
You must not be here. Stay at home with Sharid. It wil
be safer. If a soldier saw you, he might carry you off as
prisoner."

At his words, tears of fear began trickling down Jen
eum's face.

"But that won't happen," Kendall said quickly, knowing
he had frightened her. "I promise you it will never happen. I
just want you to be careful."

His words were heartening to Jeneum, but after a cold
simple meal there was no celebration or optimism in the ki-

vas that night. More than two hundred men had died that day. Fathers, husbands, brothers, cousins. Every family or clan had been affected. But there was no time for mourning. There would be time to bury the dead properly when the Spaniards had been disposed of once and for all.

"This would end much sooner," Ogath muttered, "if we could only rip their metal coats off and kill them with our bare hands."

"We can only hope that they have used up their supplies of this magic black powder that makes fire in metal sticks," Lehonti said.

"And what if there is an endless quantity?" many in the room called out. "What shall we do?"

The talk and discussion went around all evening. Midnight crept closer, and everyone was exhausted.

Gicombo made the final remarks before sending them back to their homes. "We will fight as only good warriors can: fearlessly. With strength in our great arms. And we will die the same way. Death is nothing more than a change from this world to life with the gods. But if we surrender and become prisoners, we will forever be slaves to the evil metal strangers. Death would be welcome over slavery."

Lehonti nodded, rising from his seat behind the altar. "I have spoken with the medicine men, and they agree this is the best plan. We should not permit ourselves to be taken alive. Rather than become slaves, we will kill one another. Fearlessly, and with sacred honor to return to our spirit home."

An oath was taken by all. Then the solemn oath was taken home to be shared with wives and children under each private roof.

Jeneum looked haunted when she heard about the oath. "Is there no future for us, for our family?" she asked Kendall when Akish had fallen asleep before the fire.

"Without liberty, life means nothing, Jeneum," Kendall said, but the words swelled in his throat, nearly choking him. He tried not to let his own dread show. "Please don't be afraid. Tomorrow will be better. We will beat back these evil men."

As Jeneum finally fell asleep, warmed by the fire, Kendall thought about his promise of freedom. He had to give Jeneum hope. There had to be hope for all of them. Kendall stared at the orange firelight flickering against the thick white walls. His home. How much longer would this place be his home? He couldn't think about that. He had to concentrate on surviving the Spaniards—whatever the cost might be—and helping Jeneum and Akish survive.

But he couldn't stop thinking about the fact that this battle might mean his chance of going home was gone. He might never see his father or brother again. The death oath would seal his fate forever.

CHAPTER
FIFTEEN

Early the next morning, two hundred warriors, led by Gi-combo, entered a secret cavern near the chasm cliff to lie in ambush. All the other men and boys, including Akish and Kendall, remained hidden at the village. Once the soldiers crossed the chasm, the Acoma warriors planned to rush from the cave and attack them before they could even load their weapons.

Kendall tried to imagine what the Spaniards were thinking when they rose from their bedrolls and met only deathly quiet from the village across the rock chasm.

As he and Akish crouched beneath their home's rooftop opening, Acoma appeared abandoned. Empty streets. Deserted doorways. No smoke escaping from the indoor fires. It would appear to the Spaniards as if the people had fled during the night.

The bearded Spanish general shouted orders, and the soldiers lifted heavy beams to span the crevice. Perched on the rungs of the ladder below the opening to their house, Kendall heard the call of a crow suddenly pierce the still morning. He shuddered, knowing what the signal meant.

"It is almost time," Akish whispered, standing on the rungs above him. "The strangers have begun to cross into the main village."

A moment later, Akish leaped up the ladder, and Kendall

immediately followed to join the other men in the streets. I
the distance, Kendall could see a surge of warriors swarr
from the cave and rush the soldiers with spears and arrows

The soldiers looked startled, but only for a moment. The
lifted their guns and fired the first load, taking down th
front ranks. But while they stopped to reload, the Acom
warriors ran forward, fierce in their black paint, holding club
and knives. Instantly, the soldiers drew their own swords.

Watching from the village edge, Akish let out a yell c
triumph. Finally, they had gained an advantage in going fac
to face with the Spaniards. The soldiers began to fall at th
onslaught of knives and arrows flying through the air.

The troops still on the far side of the crevice went int
action, lifting the beams so that the Acomans could no
cross over to enter their own clifftop camp. Kendall's hear
dropped as he saw that at least half of the army was stil
safely on the other side of the chasm. Those soldiers wer
able to fire and reload without fear of an advancing warrior
The Acoma men shot an avalanche of arrows across th
chasm, but most bounced off the metal armor as they had
the day before.

Kendall bit back the tears as he watched the warrior
grow more and more frustrated at how easily their brother
were killed. Rage grew, and the Acomans seethed with it
advancing toward the soldiers' guns even as their brother
were killed by the very same weapons. Kendall could hardly
bear to see these strong men lying so still on their own sa
cred earth.

A group of Acomans managed to lay another beam dowr
and raced across to fight against the soldiers, but they met a
horrible surprise.

Through the night, the small Spanish army had managed to hoist two heavy black cannons up the cliff walls by rope. Three soldiers loaded the cannons with gunpowder and shoved a pile of heavy iron balls into each yawning black mouth.

When a soldier stepped forward to light the fuses, Kendall ran in the opposite direction, screaming, "Get back! Get back!"

"¡Fuego!" came the order from General Zaldivar. The cannons' fuses were torched, and a second later, a deafening roar shattered the air.

Kendall was flattened to the ground. The blast felt like an earthquake. There was silence for one terrible moment, then screams all around him. Kendall choked on the acrid black smoke as he tried to stand and look for Akish. During the blast, he'd lost track of him. Panicking women and children swarmed the rooftops and flooded the streets. Kendall pushed himself to his feet. Then he saw the hard, round cannonball lying two inches away. Death had come too close.

The smoke began to clear, and Kendall lurched along the path, sickened to see so many Acoma warriors lying on both sides of the crevice.

Across the battlefield, Lehonti and Ogath leaped across the chasm, clubs high in the air. Kendall had never seen such hatred as the two men tried to avenge their fellow warriors' deaths. Two Spaniards rushed them with their swords, and a blade was thrust straight through Lehonti's breast. Lehonti staggered to his knees. Ogath leaped on the soldier, knocking him to the ground. The soldier rolled over, unhurt but gasping for breath, then scrambled to his feet and

quickly flashed his own blade. He raced toward Ogath an
sliced the warrior's throat.

Kendall staggered backward. Blood flowed like wate
through the streets. Kneeling behind a bush, sweat pourin
down his face, he vomited into the dirt.

Then he heard a familiar yell that made his blood ru
cold. Akish was moving toward the men who had jus
killed Ogath and Lehonti, his bow already taut with a
arrow.

"Aiiihhh," he screamed, and let the arrow fly, hitting on
of the soldiers in the arm. The Spaniard fell, crying out i
pain, and his comrade quickly knelt over him to break o
the end of the arrow sticking out of his shoulder.

Racing up to Akish, Kendall pulled him back to safet
"No more—let's get your mother and sister. We must try t
escape."

Akish's chest rose and fell. "These are the boys I playe
with as a child. These are my elders, my people. Most of m
brothers are dead, lying in their own filth upon our sacre
ground. Death to all the strangers!"

"No!" Kendall shouted. "If you keep fighting, you wil
die also. Jeneum and Sharid have lost your father, and the
don't want to lose you, too."

"But we swore an oath to die rather than be taken alive,
Akish said.

"Hasn't there been enough death? Our entire villag
reeks of it. Who will bury these people with honor?" Ken
dall lowered his voice. "Please come with me."

Amid the moaning and weeping, General Zaldivar stoo
with Tomas across the chasm.

"I urge you to surrender," came the translated words. "There has been enough killing. Surrender, and we will treat you with mercy and justice."

The remaining warriors replied with a fresh shower of arrows. Surrender in peace, after the Spaniards had killed nearly every man? More than ever, they were determined not to give their lives over to the vicious outsiders.

New wails suddenly flooded the air. Kendall jumped to his feet to look. Black smoke billowed from the rooftops of several homes.

Zoltan raced down the street, shouting, "Soldiers have invaded the village! Two rows of homes are on fire. They will kill our wives and children if we do not surrender."

Gicombo strode forward, rounding up the last of the company of men. He raised his voice. "Their leader has told us that there will be peace and mercy as soon as we give him the men who killed his brother and the others. He wants the instigators captured and brought to him."

"You call that mercy and justice?" Akish spat at Zoltan, who was standing next to him. "Must we all die to satisfy their leader's revenge?"

Empathy tugged at Kendall as he watched Zoltan put his head in his hands and weep.

There was a moment of bitter silence as they surveyed the burning village. Dense smoke poured in columns from the rooftops. Their stores of food, pottery, clothing, jewelry, and ceremonial clothing were going up in flames.

Now the roar in the village was not of cannons and guns but of a belching inferno.

Kendall took off running for home.

The entire village was in complete confusion. Smoke poured down the streets, which were littered with corpses and dying, bleeding men. Women threw themselves on top of their dead husbands and brothers, sobbing and beating their breasts.

Kendall ran deeper into the fire, choking on the harsh fumes, his thoughts only on Jeneum and her mother. As he turned the last corner, he barreled right into a group of Spanish soldiers. One grabbed him.

Kendall felt his arm being twisted painfully behind his back. Felt the man's hot breath on his face, the metal armor scrape his bare arms. Next to him, Akish was fighting the other soldiers, who were trying to bind him with rope. Akish fought like a wildcat, but within moments, both his hands were tied behind him and a soldier had whipped out his dagger to press it against the young man's throat.

Kendall's legs scraped and bruised as he was dragged to the nearest kiva and shoved him down the ladder opening. Without free hands to break his fall, Akish slid down the ladder and fell to the hard clay floor. Kendall kneeled to see if Akish was still conscious, then untied the ropes around his wrists. His Snake brother looked terrible. There was a cut above his right eye, and blood trickled down the side of his face. Akish closed his eyes against the sight of the sacred chamber.

The place was a mess. The altar had been overturned and lay broken on its side. The animal fetishes had been dumped from their jars, and cornmeal lay spilled on the floor. The stench of sweat and blood mingled like poison.

The circular room was jammed with the remaining warriors. Every one of them had been caught and thrown into the kiva.

"Why did they bring you here, boy-man?" one of the medicine men asked. "You are not one of the adult warriors."

Kendall sucked in his breath as he realized he was the only younger male in the room.

"When they saw me," Akish replied hoarsely, "they grabbed us both."

"Why have they put us in here?" another warrior asked.

Nobody seemed to know.

"At least the fighting has stopped," someone muttered.

"They want us to surrender," Gicombo said quietly.

"Is this everybody?" Akish asked.

"We are the only men left," answered the oldest warrior. He huddled against the wall, his back bent, his long hair even grayer since the fighting.

Barely a hundred men were still alive, and now they were crammed into their kiva chamber, this place used for worship and making prayer sticks. It was their place to retell the history of the people during the cold winter months. A place for their gods to visit. And now it was destroyed by the strangers, desecrated and defiled.

Kendall suddenly raised his head as the figures of the warriors standing near him began to shift and merge together. The dirt beneath his bare feet seemed to pull at his toes like quicksand. Then the room began to spin, and Kendall breathed in the overpowering smell of evil. Pressing his hands against the wall, Kendall bent over and threw up again.

The surprise made him stagger, and he dropped to his

knees, so ill he thought he'd pass out. Head reeling, Kendall recognized that this was what had happened at his initiation months ago. This was the same kiva, and he was having the same premonition of evil. This was what he'd dreamed about all summer long before traveling to the past through the enchanted passageway.

He still didn't know what the premonitions meant. He only knew that something terrible was about to happen. But what could be worse? Most of the warriors had been slaughtered. Acoma was burning to the ground even as they sat here, captured and helpless. Kendall wiped his mouth, the bitter taste of vomit stinging his throat.

A warrior leaned close. "I am sorry they have put you in here with us. Hopefully, they will spare a boy."

Akish said, "The soldiers could finish us off with one fireball thrown down the opening. The rest of the village is slowly burning, along with our women and children."

"They'll spare our wives and daughters, won't they?" someone asked.

Akish flung out his arms. "Do you think these metal strangers have any mercy in their hearts?"

Silence met his question.

Then Zoltan said, "Once we are dead, they can move onto our rock and take our women for themselves."

Everyone knew it was true. And here they were, trapped.

Kendall circled the room, prowling, unable to sit still. He was to blame for not having warned them earlier. He hadn't figured out in time what the nightmares meant. When he reached the fire pit at the back wall, Kendall stopped. Hoarsely, he shouted to the rest of the group, getting on his knees and scooping away the sand.

"If we dig here at the fire pit, we can make a tunnel into the next house. Then we can escape."

"Everyone take turns digging," the medicine man ordered.

Falling to their knees, the first group of men began to claw at the opening. Fingers were soon scraped raw, but the men took turns to create a hole in the mud and straw wall.

They were halfway through the thick wall when two soldiers suddenly yelled down into the kiva. Hands yanked one of the warriors who was standing on the ladder as a lookout, pulling him up to the surface. Kendall stopped his digging and raced over when he realized it was the oldest warrior, the man who had sat with him night after night as snakes curled in their laps. The one who had encouraged him and spoken to him like a grandfather.

Kendall crowded around the circle of daylight with the other warriors. Fear pulsed in his throat. Zoltan stood on the rungs, spying through the opening and relating the scene on the roof.

The bearded leader stood in front of a group of soldiers. He spoke sharply to Tomas, who then translated to the old Acoman warrior.

"Tell me who killed my brother Juan de Zaldivar, the Maese de Campo, along with his faithful men."

The elderly man gave a brief shake of his head.

"Who started the fight that day, and who ordered their murders?" General Zaldivar demanded.

"I don't know," the warrior said stonily.

The Spaniard made a small, quick motion with his head, and one of the soldiers standing at attention drew his sword and plunged it right into the old man's belly.

CHAPTER
SIXTEEN

The elderly Snake Runner fell to the ground, his eyes wide with shock.

Kendall heard screams from the women and children who were watching from the streets.

Zoltan shouted from the top of the ladder. "They killed him," he said, staring down at the room of warrior prisoners. "They killed him."

Before anyone could speak, the soldiers returned to the opening and grabbed Zoltan himself.

Kendall raced after them, halting halfway up the ladder rungs. Once more he heard the same question from the Spanish leader's lips, translated by Tomas into Keresan.

"Tell me who planned the murders of the men from our expedition."

Zoltan stood straight and tall, staring the leader right in the eye. "Nothing was planned."

"Tell me who killed my brother and men," the general insisted, shouting. "Or everyone in this village will pay for it!"

Zoltan eyed Tomas, then the Spanish general. Again, Zoltan said, "I don't know." Then he added arrogantly, "Even if I did—I would not tell you."

The Spanish leader flicked his eyes, and two soldiers lunged forward and ran Zoltan through with the blades of their steel swords. Zoltan fell to his knees, spat at the soldiers, then slumped into his own blood.

Kendall fell backward at the horrific sight. The Spaniards were going to kill them all in cold blood if no one confessed to the slaughter of their men.

Kendall crawled over to the men kneeling at the wall. "Dig faster. We must escape or we will all die."

He began to dig again himself, fingers splitting, bleeding. More warriors scrambled to help them, scratching and clawing at the wall. Chunks of mud and dirt fell, and at last a hole penetrated the wall into the adjoining home.

Before the first man could crawl through the narrow opening, another warrior was hauled up the ladder, kicking and fighting. When the warrior would not answer the Spaniards' questions, he was sliced in half.

At last the wall opened wide enough to let the men squeeze through. Kendall was pushed through the hole first; the rest crawled after him.

When Kendall rose to his feet in the adjoining house, he could smell himself: the fear, the bitter odor of death that lay on all of them. Any one of them could have been hauled up next to be murdered.

He didn't wait another moment, just climbed to the highest rooftop with the rest of the warriors so they couldn't be seen by the soldiers below. They leaped from rooftop to rooftop until they reached the end of the row of houses.

A moment later, Kendall heard the shouts of the soldiers as they discovered the empty kiva chamber. Pistol shots were fired into the air.

"Hurry!" Akish shouted, grabbing Kendall's arm to yank him along.

Each man ran for his own home. Kendall raced through the streets, past smoking homes, burning ladders, and the sound of fire eating its way through the village. Splashes of orange flickered against the cold winter sky. Kendall wiped a dirty arm across his watering eyes. Pouring sweat made him blind. The heat was like a raging oven. When he glanced down at his hands, he noticed the red and black war paint mixed with someone's blood. He didn't know whose blood it was.

For once Kendall couldn't seem to run fast enough. His legs felt heavy, as though weights dragged on each foot. The first row of homes began to collapse, the earth shuddering as the center house gave way, timbers burning and roof toppling.

"This is Tubaloth's house," Akish cried. "I see her in the upper rooms. She can't get out."

Kendall darted for the blackened ladder. Heat seared his face and burned the hair off his arms.

Akish pulled him back roughly. "Don't be a fool. Look, the house is gone."

Akish was right. The third story had fallen into the second. Within seconds, the middle roof gave a thunderous roar as it fell to the ground floor. Rocks and burning embers sizzled, flying through the air.

Kendall bowed his head at the sight. Tubaloth had never hurt anyone. Why were the Spaniards burning them out? What sort of revenge was this to kill hundreds of innocent people to avenge the deaths of a few uninvited visitors?

The old medicine woman was the only person who knew Kendall had come from the future. She had told him there was a purpose, a message, and he would know what that was. But he didn't know. And his last hope was now gone.

Kendall watched as the entire village died around him.

Why was he here if he could do nothing? He had come with no weapons, no power to stop what was happening.

More screams rent the air, and Kendall whirled as the row of houses behind him burst into new flames. Home after home caved in. Kendall broke into a new sprint. He was terrified at what he and Akish would find at their own home.

Akish suddenly stopped, staring up ahead. "Look, they are killing each other. Husband is killing his family, then himself."

Kendall saw what Akish saw. In the street at the end of the row, a warrior sliced the throats of his kneeling children and wife, then turned the knife on himself. Moments later, their house fell down around them.

"Death is preferred to slavery," Akish said, suddenly calm. "We must find Jeneum and my mother and do the same."

They turned the last corner to their own home, but not before seeing several men who had just discovered their families already dead fling themselves over the edge of the cliff.

"*Noooo!*" Kendall yelled, running toward the cliff edge to stop a warrior from jumping.

"Leave him to die the way he wants," Akish commanded.

As Kendall reached the precipice, the warrior leaped off. His body hung suspended in the air, then crumpled at the bottom when he hit a soft sandy dune. Kendall fell to his knees, hands swinging through empty space in a vain effort to keep the man from jumping. He watched as the warrior rolled over in the deep sand and stood up, unhurt. The man's eyes darted left then right. Kendall could practically read his thoughts. He would escape and get help from one of the villages to the east.

The man took off running, his legs swift, muscles rippling. He cleared the shadow of Sky City and headed straight for K'atzim'o, but he hadn't gone more than half a mile when the soldiers stationed on the desert floor spotted him.

"Run!" Kendall yelled to the man, willing the gods to turn the fleeing warrior invisible.

Akish appeared beside Kendall and squatted down. "Run!" he urged the man. "Run, Antelope man!"

The running warrior didn't look back, but the open desert made him an easy target. He hadn't gone very far when one of the soldiers jumped onto a saddled horse and kicked the animal into a full gallop. Swiftly closing in on the escaping runner, the Spaniard lifted his gun, took aim, and shot the warrior squarely in the back. This time the Acoman fell and didn't get up.

Kendall bowed his head, so shocked he couldn't even speak.

"It's time to leave this place," Akish told Kendall, and gently tugged at him. "We will all go to the next world together."

It seemed like it was taking forever to reach their own ladder. This was the day he should have told Jeneum to hide at the water cistern instead of staying at home. She would have been safer there, hiding under the cliff, away from the burning village.

The soldiers were quickly rounding up every Acoman they could find to stop them from killing each other. Four Spaniards reached the house just as Kendall and Akish did.

Arms dragged Kendall to the ground. He spat out a

mouthful of dirt and saw Akish wrestled to a kneeling position, two soldiers holding him down as one put a black-booted foot on his back. His Snake brother fought like a wild animal, screaming obscenities at the soldiers.

The man holding Kendall to the ground ordered rope to tie him up, but more needed to be brought from the supplies below.

The fourth soldier entered the house to search just as the homes in this last row burst into flames. A minute later, the Spaniard came out, dragging Jeneum and Sharid with him.

Kendall watched as Jeneum was roughly pulled down the ladder. He was too late to save her. He looked at her arms, dusted with cornmeal as though she had been mixing bread. Soot streaked her face.

Next to him, Akish still fought to get loose. One of the soldiers finally raised his long-handled gun and hit Akish over the head. The young warrior slumped over.

Jeneum's eyes met Kendall's, and he felt ashamed for letting her down. But her look did not berate him in the least, only pleaded to help her as the soldier holding her leered at her and put his arms around her waist, laughing.

As he watched the man's roving eyes, Kendall raised his head from the dirt and screamed at him.

The soldier holding Kendall gave him a swift kick in the back of his skull. The world started spinning, but he heard Jeneum shout his name. "K'en'dl!"

His heart seemed to tear in half at the sound of her voice. Large tears spilled down her face, and she looked at him without bowing her head, no longer shy or modest.

"Help us, please," she whispered.

For one moment, time seemed to stand still, waiting for Kendall.

The soldiers looked startled by Jeneum's countenance and the tone of her soft voice, even though they could not understand her words. As the soldier holding Kendall glanced up at Jeneum and his comrade, he loosened his hands for a fraction of a moment.

A sudden rush of power shot through Kendall's legs, and in one quick movement he was out of the soldier's grasp and on his feet. Astonishment swept over the man's face. Kendall shoved him over with both hands. The man's armor clanged as he fell backward in an awkward heap.

Jeneum leaned forward, looking more beautiful than Kendall had ever seen her. "Run like the eagle soars on the wind," she told him. "Run with the gods."

CHAPTER

SEVENTEEN

Kendall expected large, gauntleted hands to clamp down and drag him back to the ground. Any moment he thought he would feel kicks and punches or even the terrible sword piercing his side. But he ran past the burning homes to the top of the cliff trail, and he felt as though he were flying across the earth.

The soldiers' cries of rage echoed behind him, but Kendall was too far ahead to be caught now. He allowed himself one backward glance and saw Jeneum staring at him.

She looked so confident that he would escape, a faint, sad smile on her lips, her eyes drowning with tears. She trusted him completely, and for a single moment he stared at her in agony, not wanting to leave her behind, but her eyes urged him to flee. As if she knew who he was and what the future held.

He scrambled over the cliff and darted down the smooth rock paths to the large cistern. Soldiers tried to follow him, but they finally gave up, unable to move quickly in their heavy armor. Kendall disappeared among the rocks and hidden crevices like a snake slithers into his desert hole.

The burning homes became a glowing, painted backdrop against the night sky. Crouching among the boulders and rocks, Kendall thought about trying to find the distant Big River tribes to get help, but he had no idea where they were located. It would take days to run, and he wouldn't make it without proper clothing or food. If he was spotted by the soldiers, he'd be shot instantly.

A yellow moon rose as Kendall settled under the rock overhang. He couldn't stop the tears when he thought of how cowardly he must have looked to Jeneum and Akish for running away and not helping them. Running was the only thing he could do. Alone, he couldn't do anything to free them from the soldiers. He was outnumbered by men as well as guns. Jeneum had helped him escape. And she'd meant to help him, as though she'd known who he really was.

The next morning, a frigid January day, about fifty men remained alive, along with a few hundred women and children. Kendall shinnied down the cliff walls, keeping cover behind the towering rocks. Hidden behind the giant rocks on the valley floor, he watched as the last survivors were tied together with iron shackles around their ankles, then herded down the cliff to begin the walk to the distant capital village to the north.

Kendall barely recognized Akish and Jeneum and their mother, tiny figures in the long line of people, just specks among the masssive group standing in the valley between the village and the towering mesa of K'atzim'o.

The trek across the desert began. Kendall watched numbly behind the boulders, shivering in the bitter cold. The soldiers on horseback kept their guns in the air, waving them threateningly.

Hours passed as the group slowly walked out of the valley. It took most of the day, but eventually the entire line of people and soldiers vanished on the northern horizon.

endall lay across the boulders, not moving. The destruction of the village of Acoma, the complete removal of the eople, was something he never expected.

Several times over the next two days he tried to return to the top of the cliff, but he couldn't endure the sight of the ruined village. And yet he couldn't leave. He couldn't seem to do anything. He hadn't been able to help his people, and now they were gone. Would Akish and Jeneum ever return? Kendall knew he was willing to wait for them. But how long would it be? He'd wait forever. He'd wait, no matter how long it took.

Kendall wandered the base of the rock fortress, picking his way through the stones and boulders. He knew he would have to return to the village on top to see what food he could find amid the ruins. He had to eat. The cisterns were full, and he filled his leather pouch several times, living on water those first few days.

He crawled down the trail to sleep on the sun-warmed boulders. He spent hours wandering. He couldn't leave, and when he tried to run, he didn't have the heart or strength.

On the third night, Kendall found Tubaloth sitting at the base of the village trail, a small fire burning in a circle of rocks at her feet. She was dressed just as she had been the night he'd arrived at Acoma, in white deerskin, her long gray hair flowing freely around her tiny figure.

Rising from her seat on the rock boulder, she stretched her hands toward him. Kendall looked around, unsure if she was real. He'd seen her die in her own house.

"I thought you were—"

The elderly woman shushed him and stepped closer.

Kendall could almost feel the caress of her soft old finger on his cheeks, wiping the tears from his eyes like a grand mother would. But there was no flesh and bone, just the spirit of Tubaloth standing before him as she hovered be tween the land of the living and the land of the dead.

"K'en'dl," she said in the darkening twilight. "You mu run and give the people hope."

He tried to speak but couldn't. Run where? For whom Nobody was left.

"This is your message, future boy-man."

Her words startled him. He stared at the elderly med cine woman, and a smile was on her lips.

"How do you know I come from the future?"

Her voice carried clearly across the cold night wind. knew the moment I first saw you. I knew who you were an why you had come."

"But you never told me."

Her black eyes seemed to read his soul. "You came t learn the ways of your ancestors. Future generations wi spring from your seed."

"The future. I don't think it even exists anymore." Ken dall stopped, tears burning his words.

"You're wrong. Because of you the past and the futur have collided. Here. Now."

"I want to bring them all back. Akish. Jeneum. M mother."

"It's too late. Nobody can help them now."

Kendall whirled on her, grief and fear taking over. "That where you're wrong! I watched my mother die, and I won let my family die now. I won't lose Akish—I won't los Jeneum!"

Tubaloth watched him, and her expression was gentle. "Come here, boy."

Kendall slowly stepped toward her.

The elderly woman put her hands on his shoulders and looked into his face. "Your message is simple. You are the hope the people need. Acoma will never die. The people will return to live again where the gods first brought us."

Kendall shook his head, trying to understand. His felt his limbs trembling, and all he wanted to do was fall at her feet and weep his soul dry.

Tubaloth's voice was powerful, piercing. "The strangers may have burned our village and killed our warriors, but they cannot take away who we are. That's why you can never forget what happened here. Now run," she commanded. "Give your people hope. Acoma will never die. And you . . ." She grasped his arms and hands in her own, then held them to her heart. Her eyes stared into his from the depths of the spirit world. "You, K'en'dl, messenger of the gods, are living proof."

Kendall spent the night eating by the medicine woman's fire. Venison stew, loaves of bread, roots, herbs, and soft-cooked squashes poured from her never-ending pot.

In the morning, he was ready. A thin dusting of snow had fallen through the night, and the cold felt sharp. Tubaloth dressed him in warm deerskin pants and shirt, a coat made from fox, and shoes lined with rabbit fur.

"Run with the gods, who smile upon you" were her final words. "They watch and know who you are."

Kendall reached out to embrace the old woman, not wanting her to leave, but the vision dissolved as soon as he stepped forward to touch her. Gone was the fire; gone, the stew

169

steaming in the pot. But the pouch of food the medicine woman had packed inside his warm clothes was still there and still real. And Kendall knew that Tubaloth's touch from her spirit hands and the words she had spoken were also real.

Bloodstains in the snow told him the direction to run. Kendall ran all day and slept that night in a shallow cave. By mid-morning of the second day, he caught up with the caravan.

Many of the people walked barefoot. Others still wore the tattered clothes from battle. Warriors winced from dried crusted wounds that had not been tended.

Hours passed before someone noticed him running a hundred yards behind the chain of people on the desert swells. Kendall felt his heart pounding, hoping the Spaniards would not catch sight of him. Several soldiers on horseback stayed with the chained Acomans, keeping them in line and always moving. The pace was slow as they walked in tiny steps, ankles bound tightly together.

It was a group of women who suddenly recognized him. Instantly, the news spread down the line. Kendall waited and finally he saw Akish look up. He stopped in his tracks when he recognized Kendall. Not a muscle in his face moved. The young Snake warrior held his head high, and Kendall could see the bruises and cuts from the fight with the soldiers who had tied him. He limped in slow steps, iron shackles clanging, ankles rubbed raw.

Not daring to venture closer, Kendall felt his heart nearly stop beating when the soldier nearest Akish looked out to the desert to see what the Acoma man was looking at. When he saw nothing, the Spaniard impatiently shook his head, raised a whip, and got the train of people moving again.

Kendall knew Akish had recognized him, but the soldier on horseback had glanced right past him as though he wasn't even there. For days he ran unseen beside the trail of people, his people, his ancestors. The gods were watching. The ancient magic had taken over. Kendall had become a vision, just as Tubaloth had been to him, a blessing to give the people hope. Even while they were enduring the horrible evil of the metal strangers, the gods had not forgotten them.

Kendall had hoped for some kind of stronger acknowledgment from his Snake brother, but he didn't risk getting too close. Whatever fate awaited his people when they arrived at the new Spanish capital, he wasn't going to be able to help them. He was helpless to give any real aid to the suffering people. He wished it were possible to sneak among them at night and undo the iron chains. But they wouldn't be able to flee without being shot by the ever-present guards. And he couldn't release them with his bare hands.

Gray clouds filled the sky the day they arrived at the village high in the mountains, where the snows fell even deeper and the temperature was bitterly colder.

The Spaniards were living in the homes of the natives, and their women came out of the houses to stare at the large group of weary Acomans arriving in their long, shackled train.

That night, Kendall found Akish and dared to go closer.

When the camp quieted down and the midnight owls rushed through the trees, Kendall carefully approached the cluster of tents where the people had been imprisoned.

Wind howled down the northern canyons. Outside it was pitch-black, except for a handful of stars and the small glow

of a lantern next to the guard sitting outside the ten
When the guard reached for his whiskey, Kendall silentl
slid underneath the back flap of the tent.

Sleeping forms lay over the ground. The filthy, bruise
bodies of the warriors, some with toes blackened from frost
bite, huddled together for warmth.

Kendall stood still, listening to the breathing men, th
creaking of iron shackles, the leaves from the cottonwood
rustling over the top of the tent.

"Akish," he said softly.

There was an instant alertness as some of the men woke
Akish's voice came from the corner. "K'en'dl, is that you?"

Kendall skirted the sleeping forms and found Akish
hunched over, trying to keep warm. The warriors closes
to him sat up, their black eyes glittering in the darkness
They were all chained together. There was no way he could
free them.

When Kendall kneeled down, Akish reached out, care
ful not to let the metal clang. He touched Kendall's arm
"You are real, Snake brother," Akish whispered. "I though
I had gone crazy these last days and was only imagining
you."

Kendall grasped Akish's hands. "I'm real, and I want to
help you."

Akish shook his head, and Kendall noticed how matted
and dirty his hair was from so many days of walking in the
desert. His face had turned purple with bruises, and his legs
were swollen to twice their normal size. "You must be a vision because the savage strangers do not see you. How can
that be?"

"It has to be a miracle from the gods."

"If the gods want to help us," Akish said in a hollow voice, "then why has our village been destroyed and our people murdered?"

"You must not speak evil against the gods, my brother," Kendall told him. "Let us figure out a way for you all to escape."

Akish gave a short, harsh laugh. "There is no escape. Even if we could get free from these chains, those men would track us down like animals and finish us off with their fiery weapons. How much better if we had been able to die together, Sharid, Jeneum, and I. Give me a knife, brother, so that I may die now."

The words shocked Kendall, but he wasn't surprised at them.

"I should have done more to save you," Kendall said.

"Nothing could have saved us, least of all a boy," Akish replied from the darkness. "I don't know who you are, boy-man. Maybe you are just a dream. You should go back where you came from."

"Do you believe that I am Acoman?"

Akish was silent for several long moments. One of the men lying nearby gave a low grunt and shifted on the hard ground.

"I believe that you are Acoman," Akish finally admitted. "I cannot deny that."

Kendall leaned closer to his Snake brother, speaking as low as he could. "I come from a different time, Akish. Not now. Not past. A distant future."

He could feel Akish's hot breath across his face as the young man heard his strange words. Akish stared at him, and it was hard to tell whether he believed him or not.

"Tubaloth came to me three days ago. She told me that running was my message to you—to the people. The people will return to live again on our sacred rock fortress."

"I wonder if I will be among them when that time comes," Akish said quietly. "I'm not afraid to die. And I'm not afraid to be a slave. But my nightmares are ones that I don't know I can survive."

"I know your nightmares," Kendall said. "They are the same as mine."

Akish stared into Kendall's eyes. "How can that be?"

"Somehow we are connected. Through time, through blood, we are tied, but I don't know what the nightmares mean."

"You know that my greatest fear is that I will never run again. I will never feel the wind on my back and the desert under my feet as I run with my clan brothers. Now that I am bound in these chains, I know this nightmare has finally come true. That is why I no longer wish to live. It is time to die."

"Don't talk like that," Kendall said. "You can't die. You must live on."

"You realize, don't you," Akish said with a hard edge, "that most of our Snake clansmen were killed in the battles?"

Kendall knew this was true. He had watched the Snake Runners, the priests, the dancers killed by the guns and cannons. The same men he had sat with in the kiva, holding snakes and singing.

After all these months of living as brothers, Kendall knew it was time to tell Akish the secret he had been holding back. "In my time of the future, I am the last of the Snake Runners."

Akish gazed off into the darkness. "Then Tubaloth was right."

Kendall gripped Akish's shoulder and spoke closely. "Akish, you may not run again for a long time. But I need you to live so that I may exist someday."

Akish gripped Kendall's hands tightly. "You can put away your knife, runner boy. I will live for you. You came to give us all hope, not just me. You are proof that our people will someday go back after this terrible time and live again on our beautiful rock. I will return. For you and my dead Snake brothers."

"You will survive," Kendall assured him. "But the snake dances do not. They have come to an end with you in this time."

"You speak the truth?"

Kendall nodded, and he could see the pain he felt reflected in Akish's own face. His Snake brother bowed his head, and Kendall knew that Akish didn't want to believe him.

Akish lifted his head. "Then we have run and danced with our Snake brothers for the last time, K'en'dl," Akish said, and his voice broke. He swallowed hard. "When I return to Acoma—when I run in the desert alone as an old man—I will remember you."

Kendall and Akish gripped arms and stared at each other in the dark of the tent. Kendall's eyes burned, and his heart ached like he'd never felt it hurt before.

Akish whispered again, and the pain in his Snake brother's voice was something Kendall knew he would never forget. "The days of running with the snakes for the rain gods will exist only in my dreams."

Those were the last words Kendall heard Akish speak. Stomping boots outside the tent door made the entire group in the prisoners' tent stiffen. Akish embraced him so briefly Kendall wasn't sure it had actually happened.

Kendall quickly slipped out of the tent and waited for dawn.

CHAPTER
EIGHTEEN

In the morning, the plaza was made ready for the trials. Tables and benches were hauled under tent canopies, and chairs were placed beside them. Priests, lawyers, and Tomas, the translator, were given instructions for the day's events by the leader of the new capital, Don Juan de Oñate, a stocky, well-dressed older man.

Kendall stayed outside the perimeter of the village and watched from the corner of a house. The trial lasted several days.

All the events were reviewed, beginning with the expedition that had set off to explore the west and ending with their subsequent murders at Acoma. The Spanish soldiers established that when they attempted to learn the names of the murderers and sued for peace, the Acomans refused to comply and met their men with hostility and weapons. The days of battle were then outlined in detail.

On a bright, cold day in February, the Acomans were found guilty of murder. Sentences were to be carried out immediately.

The Spanish leader's secretary read the sentencing out loud to the group. Tomas interpreted for the huddling group of Acoma women and children and remaining warriors.

"In the criminal case between the Royal Court and the people of the pueblo and fortress of Acoma, accused of having wantonly killed Don Juan de Zaldivar, Maese de Campo general of this expedition, and captains Felipe de Escalante and Diego Nuñez, eight soldiers, and two servants, and of other crimes; and in addition to this, after Vicente de Zaldivar, my sargento mayor, whom I sent for this purpose in my place, had repeatedly called upon them to accept peace, not only did they refuse to do so, but actually received him with hostility. Wherefore, taking into account the merits of the case and the guilt resulting therefrom, I must and do sentence all of the men and women from Acoma under arrest as follows:

"All adult males I sentence to have one foot cut off and to twenty years of personal servitude.

"The women I sentence likewise to twenty years of personal servitude.

"All the children I declare free and innocent of the grave offense for which I punish their parents. And because of my duty to aid, support, and protect both the boys and girls, I place the girls under the care of the father commissary, Fray Alonso Martinez, in order that he may distribute them in the kingdom or elsewhere in monasteries or other places where he thinks that they may attain the knowledge of God and the salvation of their souls. The boys I entrust to Vicente de Zaldivar, my sargento mayor, in order that they may attain the same goal.

"I order that all the Acoma men and women who have been sentenced to personal servitude be distributed in the manner which I will prescribe among my captains and soldiers, who may hold and keep them as their slaves for the said term of twenty years and no more.

"This being a definite and final sentence, I so decree and order, Don Juan de Oñate."

Kendall felt a stab in the pit of his stomach like the piercing of a dagger as he finally recognized the name of the Spanish leader. One of those men was Juanita Lovato's ancestor, the one she was so proud of. And Dad had chosen to love and marry her. Kendall felt betrayed all over again. His father had betrayed his mother, too. It was something his dad could never undo.

As Tomas spoke the words in Keresan, the ragged groups of women and children standing barefoot in the square began to wail and fall to their knees on the earth.

Kendall could hardly bear the sound. The sentence that had been decreed was almost impossible to absorb. Twenty years would pass before the people would be allowed to return to their homes on Sky City and begin the process of rebuilding. The cornfields would go to ruin. What if the neighboring tribes took over the village on top of the mesa?

But even more unthinkable was the immediate future of the warriors who stood stunned at hearing what their punishment would be.

Orders were given and the soldiers complied, bringing sharpened axes and a chopping block into the center of the square. The place was crowded with people: all the Acomans, the Spaniards, and their own foreign women, as well as curious natives from neighboring villages.

The soldiers given the task of holding the first Acoma man struggled to drag him over to the block, but the warrior was helpless, still bound with iron shackles on both ankles and wrists. They pinned him down, and his right leg was tied so that he couldn't move. Another soldier raised the and brought it down across the bare flesh, deftly cutting the Acoman's foot. Blood spilled across the block, and t man was dragged off, his wild screams ripping through cold winter air.

The Acoma women tore at their long hair, pleadi for mercy in Keresan, but the Spaniards paid no attenti to them.

The next man was brought, tied, and his right foot quic chopped off. The afternoon became a horrifying specta as warrior after warrior was brought forward to face the and certain mutilation.

Kendall gripped the trunk of the tree he hid behind un the rough bark cut his palms and they bled. When Aki was taken from the group of prisoners, a soldier holdi each arm, tears burned down Kendall's face. He watch Akish's nightmare—and his own—become a reality.

The young Snake warrior was pinned down and his rig leg tied securely with rope. As the ax rose, Kendall saw Snake brother raise his eyes to the sky. He smiled a mena ing, chilling smile at his captors. The man with the ax he tated for a moment, obviously startled at the icy glare Aki gave him. Then the blood-soaked ax came down, crushi the bones in his foot as it was chopped off. Akish nev screamed. His legs jerked and he fell unconscious. Then was carried off into the crowd.

Kendall saw the Acoma women led away one by one the Spanish wives to become their servants. Each Spani woman, aristocratic in her lace shawl and full dress, pick the native she wanted for her slave. Kendall suddenly sa

Sharid, sobbing soundlessly after witnessing her son's mutilation, chosen by a petite woman with jewelry adorning her neck and hair. Still in her rags and iron chains, Sharid disappeared into one of the two-story homes.

Kendall wanted to see Jeneum. To talk to her as he had Akish. But she, along with the other younger girls and children, had been kept inside one of the houses, guarded by two soldiers. It was impossible to get near her. He felt robbed of her presence, her voice, her smile. That was all he longed for now. He hadn't seen her since the burning of Acoma. He spent the night after the sentencing trying to discover which house held the girls, but it was no use.

The next day, a group of soldiers and priests broke camp, loading their horses and pack mules. Kendall went as close as he could. Why were they packing, and where were they going?

The soldiers began to go door to door collecting the small children to place them in the wagons being prepared for the journey. When the foreign lady of the first house opened the door and handed over a little girl to a soldier, an Acoma woman suddenly raced after them screaming for her child. One by one, the children were pulled from their mothers, and the soldiers held the women back with guns and bayonets. Keresan and Spanish mingled violently, and Kendall still couldn't fathom what was happening.

And then Kendall saw Jeneum. Her arms reached for her mother, and a soldier yanked her away. Sharid fell to the snowy ground, overcome by grief.

The Spanish woman standing over her looked down helplessly, then ordered Sharid to rise. "Don't you realize that your daughter will have a better life in Mexico at the convents with the nuns?"

The small children were loaded onto the wagons to sit, and the older boys and girls were tied with rope to the rear. From his hiding place among the rocks, Kendall let out a parched cry. He raced forward, then halted in the snow. Words from the sentencing decree exploded through his brain. The children were being taken to Mexico, to where the Spaniards had originally traveled from. It was Oñate's ruling, part of the sentencing.

Even though Jeneum wasn't a young child, she was unmarried, and it must have been decided that she would go with them as well. Kendall knew she would lovingly care for the little ones and comfort them. She would also end up a slave to the nuns. He was losing her completely.

Kendall stepped out a few more paces, wanting to run to her, to rescue her, but it might mean death for them both. He had been a vision to the people during their long, cold trek, but he didn't know if the gods were still watching. He felt like he'd suddenly been deserted.

Standing in the cold, numbing snow, Kendall watched the priests climb into the wagon behind the mules. A group of soldiers took their places behind the horses, and the driver slapped the backs of the animals with the reins. The mules heaved at their bits and pulled the creaking wagons forward. Slowly, the wagon train rolled out of the village, leaving the mountain valley and heading toward the southern deserts.

Kendall leaped out from behind the rocks. Following the wagons, he ran through the tall pines, skirting the village square. He could still see her. She was tied around the waist with rope, but she had turned and was walking backward, her face to the village. Kendall knew her eyes were searching for him. Somehow she knew he was there. He couldn't stay behind the trees any longer, even if it meant the soldiers would see him. He had to let her know he was here. Stepping out from his cover, Kendall paused in the open, legs shaking with the overpowering urge to run to her.

Jeneum knew him instantly, and her chin lifted, a tremor of a smile on her lips.

She continued to walk backward, her face tied to Kendall's as strongly as the rope that bound her. Her figure was growing smaller with the distance between them, but Kendall could see her eyes as they met his across the widening gulf.

He would never forget those eyes as long as he lived. Kendall begged the gods to stretch these last few moments, to make them go on as long as possible, the final seconds he would ever see her.

As he watched, Jeneum raised her hands slowly to the sky, pressed them to her heart, then held them straight out toward him, keeping them outstretched until she was gone, disappearing over the rise in the road.

CHAPTER
NINETEEN

.

Kendall ran swiftly, sweating so badly he ended up shedding the fox coat Tubaloth had given him. Jeneum was gone to an unknown land. Akish had been taken to one of the soldiers' homes, where he would live as a crippled slave for twenty years. The family was torn apart forever.

It took Kendall only half as long to get back to Acoma as when he had followed the slow-moving caravan of chained people. Kendall hardly stopped to sleep or eat. The rabbit moccasins soon shredded, and his feet were bruised on rocks, shale, and the icy snow.

But even the running wasn't enough to heal the hole in his heart. He felt ripped apart as surely as if the Spaniards had sliced him with their swords.

When he saw Enchanted Mesa come into view, Kendall finally began to cry. The white stone citadel was still there. He'd been almost afraid that maybe something had happened to *K'atzim'o* and he'd never see Acoma Valley again. By the time he crossed the last miles of desert valley and stood at last before the great rock columns, his face and eyes were so swollen he could hardly see.

When Kendall reached the summit of the village, he was stunned to see the charred rows of houses. Piles of ash lay across the entire top of the mesa, and the blackened remains were as cold as the winter day.

Kendall slowly walked the narrow streets. Only a few empty shells remained standing. Bits of clothing, furniture, and scorched pottery lay broken among the charred timbers.

He began to run again, past the frozen bodies. There were so many of them. Kendall's breath blew like smoke as he screamed into the frigid air and raced for home—the home of Akish and Jeneum.

Fatigue made him stumble like a drunken man. His weary legs finally collapsed in front of the fallen timbers, the empty space where his home once stood. He knelt there, staring in disbelief. He couldn't move. It looked so terrible, so final.

Night drew closer, and Kendall finally got to his feet, stepping through the house's ruins. He found a few soot-covered ears of corn and set them aside to eat later. His stomach rumbled, reminding him of how little he'd eaten in the last few days.

Shards of pottery lay in a heap in front of what used to be the fire pit. A piece of bright red cloth sat miraculously unscathed under a rock. Near the front of the house where the soldiers had captured them, something under the thick ash caught Kendall's eye. Digging down into the dirt, he found Jeneum's blue stone necklace, the thin leather cord ripped in half. It must have been torn and fallen from her neck when the soldiers forced her out of the house.

Kendall brushed off the turquoise pendant, then tied it around his own neck. The necklace lay against his chest like an identical twin to the stone his great-grandfather had given him so long ago.

Holding the gemstone in his fist, Kendall stared up at

the cloudless blue evening sky and pictured Jeneum standing under the waterfall last summer. He heard her laughter. He saw her dancing in the rain. He saw her beautiful dark eyes looking at him, trusting him. Their lives had been stolen from them.

To the south the miniature mesa's white cliffs looked like pearl under the waning winter sun. A thousand miles away, Jeneum would live a far different life. She would learn a new language and be taught the strangers' religion. Possibly become a servant to a rich Spanish lady.

In a few years she would forget her own language of Keresan. She'd forget the ceremonial dances, the stories, the grinding songs that she had sung kneeling in front of the doorway during hot summer days. Those things would never be passed on through her clan or her children.

And what would she remember of K'en'dl, that strange boy who appeared out of the rock one day, the boy her brother nearly killed with his bow? Kendall would become a fragment of some long-ago dream in Jeneum's memory. Locked in the past, but having come from the future. She would never really know who he was and how much he'd loved her.

But Kendall knew. And he would never forget.

When the stars came out, Kendall huddled against one of the few standing walls. He'd seen death and destruction. He'd smelled it. He'd felt it, and he would never get over it.

"Juanita Lovato," he whispered, saying her name out loud for the first time. "You don't understand. You can never understand what happened here. You will never know, even though you think you do."

Perhaps it was her presence that had brought on the

dreams. When Juanita came into his life, she had stirred up the past, and Kendall was the only one wiser for it. She would never understand what had really happened in the past, the extinction of his own clan, the disappearance of traditions, the magical Snake Runners who could never be replaced.

But Kendall knew something else, too. Akish would come back one day a bent and broken old man. He'd be crippled, worn down by slavery. But Akish would return to rebuild the village, replant the fields, and teach the next generation. He would have children. A few Snake children. Runners to carry on a small part of the ancient past. Acoma would survive, despite everything. No one could take away that heritage, even if no one else understood it.

An icy wind blew against Kendall's face as he thought about his ancestors and the world taken away from them. If Akish could do that—could suffer the horror of amputation and humiliation of slavery and keep his hope despite it all—what a small thing it was that Kendall had to do now.

Akish had lost his family, but Kendall had one waiting for him. He still had a father who loved him and a brother who'd do anything for him. Even help him run away in the middle of the night. They weren't a perfect family; no family was. The woman his father had chosen to love was the hardest for Kendall to accept. Dad would never know why, and neither would Juanita. But they couldn't know. It wasn't theirs to know. It was only Kendall's—a knowledge that he would have to carry alone.

Kendall pressed his body against the last standing wall of Jeneum's home, trying to bear the weight of his grief.

All of a sudden the bitter winds turned soft and warm and Kendall felt something caress his face as though a hand brushed his cheek. A woman's voice whispered in his ear. "Kendall, it's time to go home."

It was his mother's voice, and he jumped to his feet, staring into the blackness.

"You have done well, my son. The gods are pleased. It's time to go home."

"Don't leave," he said.

"It's time, Kendall. Just always remember to run with all your heart."

And she was gone.

Kendall sank to his knees again. Stars glistened from the depths of the universe in the black sky above. If his mother could accept Juanita despite all that she knew . . . was Kendall supposed to do the same? It was strange to know his mother approved of what had to be, what couldn't be changed, and that she wanted him to go home. For the first time since the metal strangers had returned, Kendall felt a moment of comfort. It seemed natural that it would come from his mother. He should never have doubted that she was there, watching over him.

CHAPTER
TWENTY

In the morning, Kendall climbed down the cliff trail, his throat thick with unshed tears. At the base of the mesa, he touched the rock walls and said a prayer. Lifting his hand to his neck, Kendall felt Jeneum's stone hanging there. He wished she still had it. Without the necklace she would have no proof he'd ever existed.

The miles were slow running across the desert valley south to the miniature mesa. When Kendall got to the shale base and reached out for the magical cords, the power was as strong as ever. This time Kendall had to force himself past his own barrier that he knew he must cross to get home—because he didn't want to go.

He glanced to the north, wanting to return to Akish and nurse him back to health. Someone needed to teach him how to walk again with only one foot. Now that someone would be a Spanish master.

When he thought of Jeneum and pictured the barren desert that led south to Mexico, Kendall knew he could run to her. It would mean a trip of hundreds of miles of open land, mountains, burning sun, and very little water, but he would do it if the running would bring her back. If it could stop him from becoming erased from Jeneum's memory.

Even as Kendall contemplated the decision, he knew the power of the magic wouldn't let him go to her. The gods watched over his universe and would not allow it. He'd never make it alive. He knew that his destiny now was to take all that he'd learned—all the pain and love—and go back home.

He couldn't help Akish or Jeneum. Their fates were sealed. But his wasn't.

"Please remember me, Jeneum," he whispered to the white stone mesa kissing the winter sky above his head. "Someday I'll find you. Someday we will meet again . . . if only in the spirit world of the next life."

Kendall left the fox coat and moccasins on top of Sky City. It was cold, but he was going back to August, to summer. His other clothes were safely hidden and waiting for him.

Using both hands to hold himself up against the rock walls, Kendall took a deep breath and entered the miniature mesa's narrow crevice. Circling deeper and deeper inside the walls of the cliff, Kendall felt himself being pulled along just as he had the first time. There was the sharp, brilliant light, the never-ending pathway. All at once he stumbled out of the blackness and fell forward into the sharp shale piled around the cliff's base. His knees were scraped and blood smeared across his calves.

Kendall looked up. The valley was no different now than it had been four minutes ago, four hundred years earlier. Scrambling to his feet, Kendall hurried to the tiny crack in the mesa wall where he'd placed the prayer stick before entering the pathway so long ago.

Reaching inside the hidden spot, Kendall felt the feathers attached to the end of the snake-shaped stick. It was there, the spot no longer empty. He pulled out the prayer stick and tucked it into his leather breechcloth. Kendall let out a huge breath. He'd made it. He was really home.

Then Kendall realized his breath blew white. He was suddenly freezing. A cold front must have moved in, unusual for August. Hugging his bare chest, Kendall retraced the miles to the north, watching towering *K'atzim'o* grow closer and bigger.

He circled around to the spot where he'd hidden the duffel bag. Kendall dropped to the ground with a thud. He knew this was the place. He got up again and ran around the boulders, searching. His bag was gone. His clothes were gone. Someone must have stolen them.

Man, it was cold. His skin crawled with goose bumps, and his teeth started chattering now that he'd stopped running. A gray bank of clouds covered the sky all the way to the horizon.

Kendall started running again, hitting the two-lane road back to the highway. No cars passed, and in about thirty minutes he reached the gas station and grocery store near the exit ramp. A couple of cars and a Dodge pickup were parked in front. Kendall kept to the back of the building and started searching the garbage Dumpster for something to wear. Of course, there was nothing, just a bunch of rotten fruit and some broken crates.

A door slammed, and the pickup truck's engine revved. The vehicle pulled away, and Kendall sidled closer to the front door. He was so cold he didn't care anymore that he was wearing only his leather apron, that the rest of him was naked. When he reached the double glass doors, Kendall stopped in his tracks, and his heart began to pound like it had just gone into orbit.

His own face, taken from last year's school photo, was staring back at him from the front page of a newspaper article that had been taped to the door.

MISSING!

Fourteen-year-old Kendall Drennan of Clay Springs, New Mexico, was reported missing from his home Monday, August 12. The boy was last seen when his brother, Brett Drennan, 18, dropped him off at the road near Enchanted Mesa on the Acoma reservation near Grants, New Mexico. His older brother said Kendall was wearing shorts, Nike running shoes, and a blue T-shirt. He was carrying a duffel bag that Brett Drennan believes held Native American ceremonial clothing.

It is presumed the missing boy changed into these clothes and set off on a running expedition in the desert of Acoma Valley, but there have been no witnesses who saw the boy near this date. Kendall Drennan was last seen at the pueblo several weeks earlier during the summer ceremonies in early July.

Kendall read the article over again before he finally pushed open the double glass doors and stepped inside the food mart.

"Hey, boy," the man behind the counter called out. "No shirt, no shoes, no service. Can't you read the sign?"

Kendall's head was still reeling, and he stood staring at the man like he was mute.

The man kept arranging packs of cigarettes and chuckled, but not unkindly. "I guess you lose on all three counts."

When he didn't reply, the man turned around and gave

Kendall his full attention for the first time. "Ain't you freezin', kid? It's February, and a snowstorm's coming. Them clouds have been rolling in all morning."

"February?" Kendall repeated faintly.

"What the hell are you wearing, boy?"

Kendall glanced down at himself in his breechcloth, sash, pouch, and necklaces. His feet were black and hard as leather. His hair was uncombed and snarled from so many days of wind and running. To top it off, his stomach gave a loud, embarrassing rumble.

The man pushed his glasses back up his nose and hunched over the countertop looking at Kendall's clothing. "Is there some big powwow up on Sky City or something?"

Kendall shook his head, and his mouth started watering at the smell of hot dogs on the grill in the corner. Just seeing the soda pop machines and the shelves filled with candy bars and potato chips made his mouth salivate like crazy.

The man slapped his hand on the counter and came around to the front. "Wait a minute! Wait *just* a minute. I know who you are! You're the boy been missing from here since last summer." He grabbed a newspaper and held it up, rattling the pages until the comics section and advertisements fell fluttering to the floor. "Look, there you are on the front page today with a brand-new article."

The room spun weirdly, and Kendall slid down to the cold linoleum. "My clothes were stolen," he finally whispered.

"Your clothes?" The man rubbed his face. "Oh, yeah, they were found a few days later by the search parties. Your big brother showed the police where he dropped you off. Middle of the night, wasn't it? I've been reading the articles ever since it happened. There's been a reward offered, too."

"Reward?" Kendall gulped, and it hurt to swallow past his dry throat.

"You bet there's a reward, especially after all these months. Your daddy mortgaged his truck and put up twenty-five thousand dollars."

A strangled sound came out of Kendall's throat, and he put his head in his hands. Time had not stopped. It had been weeks, months. Dad had mortgaged his beautiful red eighteen-wheeler. . . .

The man knelt on the floor in front of him. Kendall could see his eyes magnified behind the thick glasses and could smell the coffee on his breath.

"Where have you been, boy? You've had a lot of people worried about you."

The man wanted to know where he had been. What did he say to that? There wasn't anything he could say. Nothing he wanted to say.

"Your mama and your daddy have put flyers in stores and gas stations across the state."

His mama? Then he realized the man was talking about Juanita Lovato. That was going to be hard to get used to. People assuming things, not knowing, not understanding. A rush of loss swept over him again. His mother gone, Jeneum lost across the desert and mountains of Mexico. He was still having trouble with the time change. The months he'd lost. But he'd gained another life. A life he'd never forget.

A customer came in and the man turned, holding up his hand. "Be right with you," he called. Then his voice grew tender. "Tell me what happened, son. Were you kidnapped? Did something terrible happen?"

Kendall stared at the floor through blurry eyes. His chest urt. His heart hurt. He felt panic rising in his stomach. "I asn't kidnapped. How do you know so much?"

"It's been in all the papers. Why, your big brother blames imself. Missed the first week of college because he was search-g all over this valley for you."

Another customer clanged the bell, and the gas-station wner got to his feet. He retrieved his own jacket and let endall wear it while he rang up the woman's sale, then he turned with two hot dogs smeared with mustard and a big up of Coke.

"Now you eat that while I call the police," he told Kendall.

"No!" Kendall said, suddenly comprehending what the an was saying. Adrenaline shot through his body. "Don't all the police."

"But everybody's going to be so happy that you've been und." The man lowered his voice. "Was it that terrible?"

Kendall stared at him, trying to figure out what he meant. t was terrible," he finally said softly, looking away. "And it as wonderful."

The store owner frowned, then shook his head in bewil-erment. "Those kidnappers got your head pretty messed up."

Kendall's mind was racing forward, then back again. Could you give me some change for a phone call, sir? I'll ay you back."

The man stared at him and scratched his chin. "Well, ure. You probably want to call home. That's a good idea. hat's exactly what you should do. You call your daddy right way." He went behind the counter and opened the register.

The coins felt cool and hard in his palm. Kendall walked

down the aisle to the pay phones lined up along the back wall. He picked up the black receiver, tried to deposit the first quarter, dropped it, scraped it off the floor, then finally got in the slot and dialed. He heard the line ringing and gripped the side of the phone booth until his knuckles whitened.

He didn't even know what day of the week it was. Would Dad be around, or was he out on a long haul across the country? He couldn't imagine Juanita printing flyers and taping them up in grocery stores.

Kendall wanted Dad to answer the phone. But maybe that wasn't such a good idea. His father would have a police helicopter flying right over to pick him up. Crowds, television cameras, reporters in his face. Maybe Brett should answer the phone. After all, Brett had dropped him off that night. He felt guilty about what he'd put his brother through.

Kendall soon realized the phone had been ringing and ringing. Nobody was home after all. He didn't know whether to hang up or keep waiting. Should he let the phone ring a hundred times, a thousand even, until somebody got home? Then, suddenly, the receiver was snapped up, and Brett's voice came on. He was out of breath, like he'd just run inside the house.

At the same moment, Dad picked up on the other extension, and Kendall heard them say hello at the same time.

He couldn't speak. Just hearing their voices made his throat close up so tightly he couldn't even breathe.

"Hello?" they both said again. "Hello, anybody there?"

Slow seconds of silence passed as Kendall tried not to burst into tears.

Then Dad, his voice turning husky and faint, finally said, "Guess they hung up."

"I don't know," Brett said. "I never heard a click."

Kendall was dying to say something, but he knew suddenly that he wasn't ready. It didn't feel right to wait here while they jumped in the car and tore down all those miles of highway to get him. Dad would start crying, they might get into an accident. They'd probably call the police before they left the house, too.

Officers would be swarming this truck stop in ten minutes. Police detectives in his face, asking questions. They'd want to take him to the hospital for tests and stuff. But Kendall wasn't going to any hospital. He wanted to go home. After trying to stay in the past for so long, now that he was back, he was going home—nowhere else.

Besides, what could he tell anyone about where he had been that would make any sense? One of the most difficult things he'd ever done in his life was to watch Jeneum disappear with her captors over the desert, longing to run to her and rescue her. This was nearly as hard. Kendall slowly hung up the phone and leaned against the wall. He sucked in his breath and knew he'd better get moving before he lost his nerve.

Keeping his eyes on the man at the cash register, Kendall took off the man's jacket and laid it on the end of the counter. He moved slowly along the aisles until he reached the double glass doors and started to push his way through.

"Hey! You can't leave," he heard the man shout behind him. "We gotta call the police."

Kendall slammed the door and began to run. He sped

around the back of the building, past the gas pumps, past customers staring stupidly at him, and leaped down the arroyo into the sagebrush, almost falling on the skittery rocks at the bottom.

There was the path that led to the desert. The February temperatures were freezing, but he'd soon warm up.

Hidden by the brush, Kendall slapped his thighs to warm up, then brushed the long hair out of his eyes. He was sunburned, tough and leathery, and he knew he could do it. He'd run for more than a week through snow and lonely, empty canyons. It would be tough but not impossible, and he'd probably arrive by nightfall.

Cupping his hands, Kendall picked up the two stone necklaces hanging around his neck and gently kissed them together.

He had to make the final leg of his journey home alone. Just him and the desert and the gods, the spirit of Jeneum gathered safely inside his heart, and Akish, the last of the ancient Snake Runners, by his side.

It wasn't much more than fifty miles.

It would be an easy run.

AUTHOR'S
NOTE

The historical events in *The Last Snake Runner* are true. The account of the battle at Acoma is found in a record written by one of the soldiers, Captain Gaspar Perez de Villagra, who was in the actual party that laid siege to Acoma in January 1599. Captain Villagra published an account of these tragic events in 1610, several years after the expedition and his return to Spain. This book was later translated into English and gives us a first-person account of this extraordinary time.

There may be readers who wonder if these horrific events are exaggerated. It is evident that my story is told from a point of view sympathetic to Native Americans, but the details of the battles and the ensuing events are taken directly from the writings of this Spanish soldier, who was an eyewitness. Europeans living in the sixteenth century had a completely different view of other nations and cultures than we do today. The Spanish conquistadors were on an expedition that was deeply important to them, a mission given to them by their king and queen to discover new lands and spread the gospel of Christianity. Obviously, people and cultures are going to clash. Lack of communication and a lack of understanding between two vastly different cultures led to many of the unfortunate events that happened to the Acomans and to the other Southwestern tribes during this time period.

Don Juan de Oñate, the leader of this huge expedition, had to make difficult decisions, often without firsthand knowledge. Some of his decisions were, regrettably, vicious. He was later brought to trial in Spain, banished from New Mexico, and fined a great sum of money.

Today there are still deep feelings of pain between the native tribes of New Mexico and Spanish descendants. Many people want to revere Don Juan de Oñate as a great explorer. Memorials have been erected. Understandably, the Native Americans do not want him honored.

Readers may also be curious about the unusual snake dance ceremony portrayed in this story. Today the snake dance is performed only at the Hopi reservation in eastern Arizona. None of the pueblos along the Rio Grande in New Mexico or at Acoma pueblo have performed it for centuries, but there is definitely evidence that these rites and dances were a part of these tribes' culture.

Some of the last living Snake Runners at Acoma were photographed in 1906. The last member of the Snake Clan at Acoma, an elderly man, died in the 1920s. When the village of Acoma was destroyed in January 1599, most of the warriors were killed during battle, and the few remaining men had their feet amputated. These tragic events marked the end of the snake dance ceremonies, as well as the beginning of the death of the Snake Clan, which is now extinct.

The depiction of the snake ceremony is taken from several sources written by historians and ethnologists during the last hundred years. For the sake of portraying this unique ceremony succinctly, I had to condense and simplify this sixteen-day event with its many rituals, songs, dances, and prayers. There is no way to do it proper justice, but my efforts have been made with deep respect and admiration for the Hopi and Acoma nations. I hope that the reader will also view it respectfully and will recognize the sacredness of this deeply religious ceremony.

I have visited the pueblo of Acoma many times and have personally felt the ancient, wondrous magic of its desert citadels. In such a deeply spiritual setting, I wanted to bring to life a modern boy of mixed parentage and the dramatic way in which his fears, challenges, and dreams are affected by the events of his ancestors. When we dare to look back on our history and roots, the ties that link us to the past, present, and future are remarkably revealed.

ABOUT

THE

AUTHOR

Kimberley Griffiths Little has received accolades for her well-researched fiction. She is the author of two additional novels, including another featuring Kendall, *Enchanted Runner*, which was published by Avon Camelot in 1999 and received the Southwest Book Award. A voracious reader who grew up in the San Francisco Bay area, she now lives with her three boys and her husband, a robotics engineer, in a solar adobe house along the banks of New Mexico's Rio Grande. This is her first book for Knopf.